Advance Praise for *Midnigh*

"Tara Campbell's stories exist a
to the left from our world—p
into lions, and hearts are sold in the mall—while simultaneously beautifully and deftly exploring exactly what it means to be human."

Tina Connolly, World Fantasy-nominated author of
On the Eyeball Floor and Other Stories

"So much unexpected happens in Tara Campbell's weird and wonderful short story collection, *Midnight at the Organporium*, that I didn't want to let these stories go. This slim, but packed collection of 12 stories makes the ordinary extraordinary—from the ghost of Lucille in "Death Sure Changes a Person" to a thief of hearts in the Southside Mall in the title story, "Midnight at the Organporium." Red from Red Riding Hood re-tells her story with a roar and a vengeance in "Another Damn Cottage." Whereas, "You, Commuter," is a nightmarish wonder of flash fiction about an everyday bus ride. "The Rapture" comes at you slant, or at least that's how it opens, and we soon have much more than a commonplace end of the world story—we have a story of race that rises on the shoulders of Octavia Butler. These stories all astonish and astound. From full-length to flash fiction, Campbell's stories in *Midnight at the Organporium* sneak up on you with an exquisite hyper-realism, a sure-fire wit, and most of all, a daring sense of adventure and possibility. "

Caroline Bock, author of *Carry Her Home*,
Before My Eyes, and *Lie*

"Sometimes funny, sometimes frightening, and always full of heart—in *Midnight at the Organporium*, the everyday and the fantastic conspire to create the authentic."

Erin Fitzgerald, author of *Valletta73*

Midnight at the Organporium

Conversation Pieces

A Small Paperback Series from Aqueduct Press
Subscriptions available: www.aqueductpress.com

About the Aqueduct Press Conversation Pieces Series

The feminist engaged with sf is passionately interested in challenging the way things are, passionately determined to understand how everything works. It is my constant sense of our feminist-sf present as a grand conversation that enables me to trace its existence into the past and from there see its trajectory extending into our future. A genealogy for feminist sf would not constitute a chart depicting direct lineages but would offer us an ever-shifting, fluid mosaic, the individual tiles of which we will probably only ever partially access. What could be more in the spirit of feminist sf than to conceptualize a genealogy that explicitly manifests our own communities across not only space but also time?

Aqueduct's small paperback series, Conversation Pieces, aims to both document and facilitate the "grand conversation." The Conversation Pieces series presents a wide variety of texts, including short fiction (which may not always be sf and may not necessarily even be feminist), essays, speeches, manifestoes, poetry, interviews, correspondence, and group discussions. Many of the texts are reprinted material, but some are new. The grand conversation reaches at least as far back as Mary Shelley and extends, in our speculations and visions, into the continually created future. In Jonathan Goldberg's words, "To look forward to the history that will be, one must look at and retell the history that has been told." And that is what Conversation Pieces is all about.

L. Timmel Duchamp

Jonathan Goldberg, "The History That Will Be" in Louise Fradenburg and Carla Freccero, eds., *Premodern Sexualities* (New York and London: Routledge, 1996)

Conversation Pieces
Volume 67

Midnight at the Organporium

by
Tara Campbell

Published by Aqueduct Press
PO Box 95787
Seattle, WA 98145-2787
www.aqueductpress.com

10 9 8 7 6 5 4 3 2 1
ISBN: 978-1-61976-163-6

Prior publication history, p. 110.

Cover illustrations:
Pond background, © Can Stock Photo / Antikainen
Heart, © Can Stock Photo / focalpoint
Vine, © Can Stock Photo / nanDphanuwat2526

Original Block Print of Mary Shelley by Justin Kempton:
www.writersmugs.com

Printed in the USA by Applied Digital Imaging

Acknowledgments

So many people have been part of this menagerie of stories, but I'll start with special thanks to Michele Lerner and Dorothy Reno for inviting me into their writing communities, and for all the writers they gathered together over the years: Carrie Callaghan, Andrea Pawley, Beth Wenger, Raima Larter, Jeanne Jones, Stefen Styrsky, Mary Sophie Filicetti, Jessica Siegel, Nick Mandle, Josh Trapani, Dave Todaro, and Diana Veiga. It has been a blessing to work with and learn from these writers, and to have their advice and encouragement. The DC-area literary community is incredibly rich, and I'd like to thank Lacey N. Dunham and Tyrese Coleman as well for organizing additional groups from which I've benefitted—thank you!

Much love to the Barrelhouse fam and to the American University MFA community for all of their support. I am also indebted to the following people for their roles in my literary journey: Carrol Fix, Richard Agemo, Bridget Grimes, Amber Sparks, Rion Amilcar Scott, Laura Ellen Scott, Jan Elman Stout, Jane Carman, Kathy Fish, Dave Housley, Tara Laskowski, Gay Degani, Tina Connolly, Erin Fitzgerald, and Caroline Bock. And, of course, it has been a treat to work with L. Timmel Duchamp and Kath Wilham on this collection!

And to my husband Craig Hegemann: thank you for your unwavering belief in my work, and for giving my menagerie room to thrive.

Contents

Death Sure Changes a Person

The first time I saw Lucille after she died, she told me, "You better find someone new, Harlan, or you'll be lonely."

Needless to say, I was surprised. Just three weeks after she'd passed on, here was the world's most jealous woman telling me I should run out and start dating someone new.

"I don't know what I expected over there," she went on, "but it wasn't this. Everyone is with everyone they've ever *really* been with. I don't mean flings, but the people you actually loved. Even if you wouldn't have wanted to share that person with anyone else, it's okay, because they're sharing you with everyone else too." She flung her hands out, supposedly gesturing at the piles of people sharing each other around her. "I mean, not everyone," she backtracked. "We've still got some standards. But it doesn't matter anymore, is what I mean."

So by now you might have guessed that Lucille, unlike me, had had a normal love life. By the time we met, most folks had been through a marriage or two; but me, I'd just been chugging along on my own. Not like I didn't want to be with anyone. But I was quiet in a loud world, as my mother put it. Didn't get out much. Lucy on the other hand had had her loves and affairs by the time we got together, which didn't bother me really. She never talked about the others that much, and when she did they were more like milestones in a previous life than flesh and blood men I'd actually have to worry about.

"I lived in that part of town when I was married to Mike," she'd say. Or, "I was in Cancun once; Joe took me on his miles." She didn't say too much more about the men in particular, and I didn't really need to know more.

Sometimes, back when she was alive, she'd get this faraway look in her eye, and I'd wonder what she was thinking about, if she was back in that little house on the other side of town or on the beach in Cancun. I asked a couple of times, and she'd just say, "Nothing," and then busy herself with something else like dishes or laundry or checking if the bird feeder was full, and then she'd be further away than before. So I stopped asking, 'cause like I say, I didn't really need to know. It could honestly have been nothing, like she said. Or maybe it really was something, more than she wanted to talk about; like maybe she was wondering if she should have stopped to have children somewhere along the way. Wasn't in the cards by the time we met.

Anyway, the first time I saw her after she died, it was really bad timing. It was a few weeks after we'd laid her to rest, as I mentioned, and I was ready to get back to work. The shop would have let me stay home longer, but my hands needed a car or truck to tinker on, even if I was tired as hell most of the time. I still wasn't sleeping right, seeing her in my dreams and waking up. She'd be lying next to me in the dream, asleep, and I'd get this feeling like *thank God*, and pull her close.

She never let me spoon her when she was living. She didn't want me feeling her belly, which she thought was too soft—but who doesn't have a little extra padding by this side of fifty? I didn't care. If I woke up while she was sleeping, I would scoot over behind her and hold her as close as I could without waking her up. Her hair always smelled so good, clean and warm, not too full of perfume. I'd squeeze her, tight, so hard she'd know how much I loved her, but without waking her up.

But now I was the only one waking up, clutching nothing but a mangled pillow.

So the first time I saw Lucy after she died, I was just trying to get myself back into the shop, and it was morning, and I hadn't slept well. I was kind of floating in and out before my alarm was set to go off. I'd been dreaming I was holding her, and that time I couldn't help it, I just squeezed her so hard she wouldn't be able to breathe, much less stay asleep. And then I heard, "Oh, Harlan, let go of my belly." Not bossy, mind you, but shy. Embarrassed. It was her voice, her soft, sleepy mumble, and it made me want to cry, because the thing is, I never saved any of her messages. I didn't have her voice anymore. You never think about that when you have the chance. You don't realize that's your chance.

I heard her voice again and woke up, and then she was turning in my arms, and sitting up against the headboard, and looking at me like she was actually there.

I sat up slow, not wanting to lose this part of the dream, and that's when she told me, "You better start dating, Harlan."

Of course I didn't know what to say, which was okay because she did all the talking. That's when she told me how it was where you go after you go. She didn't call it heaven or the afterlife or anything like that. She called it "over there," I think because she wasn't quite sure herself, being new and all. There wasn't really any kind of orientation, you just woke up from whatever event brought you there (car accident in her case), and there were the people you cared about most, *whether they were dead or not*, even those who had moved away, or those you hadn't thought about in a while.

You were just all together, eating or singing or dancing or exploring ruins or hiking, whatever you liked to do most. It was like a mashup of all your favorite memories, even if they didn't happen that way.

I found that part out when she told me about going to Macchu Pichu with Rod.

I'd never heard that name before. "But wait," I said. "Aren't these supposed to be memories?"

"Yes," she said, examining her fingernails.

It seemed a little ridiculous to press her about Rod at that point, so I asked, "But you never went to Macchu Pichu, did you?"

"No, but Rod and I always talked about it." She shook her head, still looking at her nails. "I don't know why I spent all that time painting these things." She sighed and looked at me. "I want you to have this kind of life when you get over here too."

"But I thought I was already over there with you. You said everyone you cared about was over there." That meant everyone, ex-husband, past boyfriends, family, everyone. Including me.

She shrugged and picked at the quilt. "Yeah, you're there. But…"

"But what?"

"Well, I've got a lot going on over there, and you're just kind of…" She shrugged again. "I see you sometimes, standing off on the—what's that word, on the side?"

"On the periphery." Popped right out of my mouth. I'd been looking at that entry on her little "Word of the Day" calendar every morning since her accident.

"Right, 'on the periphery.'" She took my hand. "But you deserve better, baby. You need to experience more things *here*, because then you'll get more out of life over *there*. I don't know, travel, sing, dance, bungee jump, anything. You just need to get more to draw upon *now*, to last you *then*."

I didn't know what to think, her looking into my eyes, her hand so soft and solid in mine. Why would I want to go anywhere else with her back here at home? All I could think to do was mumble something about the job I had to stay for, the funeral expenses I had to pay off. I felt bad as soon as I said it, and she looked hurt.

"I always told you to just burn me up."

"I did. You're right over there." I pointed toward an urn on the dresser. "It costs more than you think."

She stared at the urn for a moment, then looked down at the quilt in thought. "Well, you don't actually have to travel, if you don't want. Whatever you do, you just have to want it. Really want it."

I must have looked dubious, because she squeezed my hand and said, "It doesn't have to cost anything."

My heart clutched right then. She really knew me.

"Just live," she said. "What do you want?"

I kept looking right at her.

"I mean," she said softly, "aside from me. Is there anyone else?"

I shook my head.

"Come on," she said, a little smile weaving its way into her lips. "Isn't there anyone else you've been thinking about?"

I could feel myself blushing. "Come on, now, it hasn't even been a month."

"I know, but don't you want to hold someone? Kiss someone?"

Sure, and she was sitting right in front of me. But Lucy went and misinterpreted my look.

"See, I knew it," she said. "I understand. You're a man; you have urges. I *want* you to."

"You want me to…" I couldn't even finish the sentence because I couldn't imagine anyone I'd want to finish it with but Lucille.

But she said, "Yes. I mean… Yes, I want you to love someone again." She let go of my hands. "Someone else."

And just like that, I was sitting there with my hand gripping nothing, the quilt deflating from the sudden departure of her shape.

I couldn't believe it. Here my wife comes back for a good half hour, and spends it telling me to go out there and forget all about her. When she was alive she would always try to trip me up, figure out if there was anyone else in, say, the past few decades before we met that she should be worried about. Seems she was finding out now that I'd always been telling her the truth.

Well, I called in sick and waited for her to come back. Half the day was gone before I started to feel cooped up and had to go out for a walk. Sidewalks around here are pretty non-existent, and I was pretty out of it, so it's a miracle I didn't get hit—although truth be told, maybe that's kind of what I was going for.

In fact, I almost had a scrape that day with Beverly's cherry red '68 Mustang hardtop convertible, though I didn't know Beverly's name at the time. I can only assume there was some kind of divine guidance going on because (1) I didn't get mowed down and (2) a woman as cute as her in a car like that actually stopped and said hello. Not at first, though. At first it was "Sir, would you mind stepping out of the middle of the road?"

She'd stopped with more than enough room to spare (believe me, the worst accidents we see in the shop are not from women drivers), then crawled up to me in that 'Stang real leisurely, and popped her head above the windshield to ask if I weren't interested in getting out of the way.

I turned around and stared at her, still as a stump, and here's where divine guidance struck again because (3) she didn't call the police. She could see how bad I was hurting, and asked me where I had to get to, and when I said I didn't have anywhere in mind, she told me well come on then and go with her to Bingo.

I didn't know what to say.

"Or does the man standing in the middle of the street have a better idea?" she asked. So I got on in the car.

I kind of play-scolded her about letting strange men into her car, but she told me I wasn't a complete stranger. She did nails at my cousin Margot's beauty salon, where I got my hair cut (it's unisex, mind you). Margot had given me a haircut the day before Lucy's memorial, which was how Bev knew I could probably use a lift right about then.

It turned out Bingo was at her father's nursing home and was just the kind of mindless activity I needed. I even won a coupon for a free Domino's pizza, delivered, which I gave to her daddy; which, she told me later, was her sign that I'd been worth picking up. I was almost afraid to go home after Bingo 'cause of the nice time I'd had so soon after laying Lucy to rest. Well, Bev asked did I want to talk about it, and while I didn't want to wallow in all that, I didn't want to go home either. So we went for a coffee. Felt kind of like a traitor, even though I guess that's what Lucille wanted to happen. I'll never know how women always wind up in control.

I didn't dream about Lucy that night, and she didn't come back the next morning. I spent my first day back at the shop dropping wrenches and bumping into waste barrels and tire racks. Just glad nobody saw me almost drop a car off the lift. Thing is, I was expecting to see Lucy's face in my mind—I didn't expect to see Bev's. Or think about her laugh. Or feel that same crazy-good gut-squirm I felt when she revved up her Mustang.

Sure, I looked at the number Beverly had saved on my phone, but I didn't call her that day. Or the next. And a third day was slipping by in the same manner when Lucy appeared with folded arms and a frown and said, "Come on, Harlan, would you call her already?"

Well, and there was the paradox, see? I couldn't call Bev with Lucy standing right there, but I wouldn't call her otherwise. Lucy had to threaten me with a regular old haunting to get me to do it. And she'd never been one for idle threats: she came back the following night bearing a hatchet and knocked some stuff off the shelf, and even though I knew (or didn't think) she'd really hurt me, I figured it also wouldn't hurt to get on the horn to Bev the next morning. We made a date for the following week.

Then a couple of hours before the date, Lucy came back to make sure I wouldn't chicken out. She said the me over there—the place she'd started calling "Now"—was rooting for the me over here—the place she now called "Before." She said the other me, Now-me, was really hoping I'd hit it off with Bev.

"I know it seems early," she said. "And if I were still here with you, I'd think you were a pig. But I know better now." She chuckled. "I guess death sure changes a person." She cupped my face in her hands. "Harlan, I want you to get out there and fall in love again. Don't waste your Before just sitting around missing me, because in the Now you'll have me forever."

Well, by then I was too confused to say no. And honestly, as ashamed as I was to admit it, I was actually looking forward to the date. I told myself it was partly about wanting to ride in the 'Stang again, but deep down I knew better. Then I told myself I was mostly doing it to please Lucille, but I knew that was a bunch of bull too.

Simply put: I was really looking forward to seeing Beverly again.

As to where we'd go, Bev had said she wanted to surprise me. Said it was somewhere she'd been wanting to go for a while and she hoped I'd like it too. I assumed it'd be something like a wine tasting or some garden show like Lucy was always dragging me to. But doggone if she didn't surprise me by taking me to the go-cart track. What a hoot, Bev and me and all those kids zipping around the circuit! She whooped every time either one of us plowed into a tire-lined wall. We topped it off by going for burgers, and she ordered a boozy milkshake that turned out to be about the size of her head. So I helped her finish it, and then out came the coffee and the corny jokes while we waited for her head to clear. And by the time she dropped me off, my face was sore from smiling.

Well, things went on like that, and people started talking, but Bev and I didn't care. We were happy, and despite everything, I felt at peace 'cause I knew I had Lucille's blessing. She said as much when she came to visit me a few weeks later.

I was in the bedroom one evening after work, getting ready to go over to Bev's. I'd just slipped into my birthday suit and was about to head for the shower when I heard the water turn on. Well, I walked into the bathroom, and guess who I saw there, wrapped in a bitty pink bath towel with her hair pinned up.

"Hey, darlin'," said Lucille. "I'd ask how you're doing, but I can already tell things are going gangbusters over here. Over in the Now you're positively beaming. The way Now-you's talking, your Now-Bev could show up any minute." Then she gave me this sexy little smile and looked me up and down. "What say we celebrate?"

Well, I'm not ashamed to say I was tempted. She was my wife and all, even if she was dead. But I had somewhere I wanted to get to, so I gathered up all the willpower I had and told Lucy I was kind of in a hurry just then.

Then she got this surprised look, though I thought that might be for show, since she seemed to know ev-

erything going on in my life already. "Oh, you got somewhere else you got to be?"

"Well, you see, Bev's waitin' on me and—"

"Now, now, I'm sure she'd understand a poor wid-
ower needing a little time to himself." Then she winked
and let her teeny pink bath towel slip to the floor. Death
hadn't diminished her curves one bit.

Now, I'm no apologist for necrophilia, but at that
moment I was wondering how closely this circumstance
fit the generally accepted definition of the act. And judg-
ing from his reaction, little Harlan didn't seem to mind
either way.

The shower was running hot, real hot, with steam bil-
lowing out from behind the curtain. The humidity was
almost targeted, coaxing me to relax, conspiring with
everything else to loosen my resolve. Still, I managed to
stammer, "I'm sure I'd be just as happy to celebrate with
you over there, in the Now."

And that's when it happened. Her face went from
sexy to sour and back again, so quick I almost missed it.
She paused for a second, then cocked her hip and raised
an eyebrow. "You're already happy over there. Don't you
miss me over here?"

She stepped over to me, and I could barely breathe.
Steam had begun to curl the loose hair around her face
into those ringlets I loved. Moisture beaded on her skin.
She looked up at me, heavy-lidded and sure of herself—
of us. I wanted to reach out and touch the drop just
beginning to form at her collarbone, follow it down to
her breast.

But she wasn't real. I don't know where I got the
strength, maybe it was that other me over in the Now

rooting for Bev, but I backed right out of that bathroom and closed the door. I'd love to pretend that's the only thing I had to do to *relieve the tension*, shall we say, but I was a man, and Lucy was still in great shape, so I had to take independent countermeasures to clear my head.

By the time I got myself situated again, the shower had turned itself off. I opened the bathroom door. The room was empty. Still, I called Bev to see if she minded my showering over at her place. And she said only if I didn't mind her joining me.

Well, we went on like that, me and Bev, week after week. It was that floaty, magical beginning part, you know, where you felt like you were invincible, and anything that could have struck you down before was a mere bug bite now. Days at the shop flew by; all the repairs seemed easy. The guys started ribbing me, calling me the Florence Nightingale of cars—and I didn't even mind. Nothing could slow me down, you know?

Which was probably why I wasn't more worried about what was going on with Lucy. She started coming back more often, sometimes wearing a tight dress, or negligee, or a cheerleader outfit, even one time a full-on pleather dominatrix suit. She tried on different personas with the outfits too, sometimes sweet, sometimes sultry, or funny, or bossy; she tried a bunch of stuff. Just playing, she said. At first she'd come once a week, then a couple of times a week, then every day. I suppose I thought her coming back was just some sort of grieving process on my part—an unusually vivid, insistent grieving process. I started spending more time at Bev's because Lucy never bothered me there. But I didn't even realize—or admit to myself—I was going over there as much to get away from Lucy as to bask in the glow of my new romance with Bev.

So the last time Lucy came by to visit, it was about four months after I'd laid her to rest. She came into the bedroom one night as I was getting ready for bed—Bev and I had decided to have an evening apart for a change. She wasn't in any get-up that time, just a T-shirt and jeans like she always wore before. I was mighty relieved to see the sane, kind, no-nonsense Lucy I'd always loved—until I noticed the shotgun slung over her shoulder.

My throat clenched.

"I know what's going on," she said, mournfully shaking her head.

I slid my hands stupidly over my pajama pants, wishing I was still wearing jeans with pockets to keep my hands from shaking.

"Harlan, I know you, and that's why I'm here: to save you from yourself."

"Well gosh, honey." I cleared my throat and held my voice steady. "I probably wasn't in any kind of danger until you walked in here with that gun."

"I'm sorry to shock you, Harlan, but I know what's about to happen. You're going to ruin everything!"

"Now, darlin'—" And there I had to stop myself, because I knew the best way to get her even more riled up was to tell her to calm down.

"Nope, too late to sweet talk your way out of this. You're about to get cold feet with Bev and try to back out so as not to get hurt. Why else would you be here tonight, alone?" She blinked back the tears welling up in her eyes. "I tell you, the Harlan over there in the Now

is already sick about it. So I'm not gonna let it happen."
Then she leveled the shotgun at me.

But suddenly, despite how steady she pointed those
double barrels at my chest, I wasn't afraid. Because I
knew I didn't have the problem she was trying to fix.

"Lucy, darlin', that's not gonna happen. I learned my
lesson. I learned it with you."

And that was the god-honest truth. Why hadn't I
thought of it before: I'd been an idiot a few months into
my courtship with Lucille. I panicked about getting seri-
ous and tried to slink away like a dog in the dark. And I
bet she wished she'd had a ghost with a shotgun to make
me see sense instead of having to go through all that
drama and pain, losing me and then having to decide
whether to risk loving me again when I crawled back and
asked her to forgive a colossal fool.

She shook her head and gripped the gun tighter. "I
know you, Harlan. You think you're in love, but that's
just the rebound talking. I'm not gonna sit by and watch
you realize you never really cared about that woman. It'll
break Now-Harlan's heart."

"Baby, it's not like that. I'm not gonna chicken out."

A tear spilled down Lucy's cheek and the shotgun
shook in her hands.

"Lucy, honey, don't worry." I held my hand out to
her, pleading. "I love Beverly too much to leave."

And that's when the gun went off.

I'll tell you right now, it's not like what they show on
TV, when everything shifts into slow motion and you
have that high, whiny feedback sound in your ear; or
everything fades to washout, or just plain cuts to black.
Well, maybe there's an instant of suspended time before

you process what happened. But mostly, it hurts like hell. All you can do is squeeze your eyes shut and clutch your chest and think, "Shit!" or maybe, "Holy shit!" if you're the religious type.

Next thing I knew, I was waking up in bed next to Lucille. I rubbed my eyes and tried to sit up, which was when I discovered my chest still hurt like the dickens, so I had to lie back down. I looked around the bedroom, bright with mid-morning light slanting through the blinds, and then up at Lucille. She was sitting up against the headboard with a book in her hand, looking down at me.

She smiled and said, "Some night last night, huh?"

That was about the time I remembered she'd shot me. I patted the bedside table for my phone, ready to dial 9-1-1.

"It's not there, Harlan," she said. "We don't need them over here. In the Now." She put down her book and slipped under the covers beside me. The slightest touch of her hand on my chest made me wince. "Ooh, sorry babe. I was in rough shape too when I first got here, but the pain'll go away in a couple of weeks."

"What the—does that mean I'm—"

"Yes, darlin'. You're dead. But only in the Before. Here in the Now, you're forever." She rested her cheek on my shoulder. "We're forever."

I lay there quietly and gave that grenade time to explode inside my head. I thought about how bad I felt about Lucille when she passed, and then I thought about how bad Bev was going to feel when she found out I'd passed.

Lucy's voice vibrated against my shoulder. "I'm real sorry, Harlan. I just couldn't let you mess things up for Now-us."

"Well, I don't know about this."

"Don't worry, baby, no one will think it's suicide. I made it look like a robbery gone wrong."

"That's not what I—thanks, by the way—but I was thinking about Bev."

Lucy kind of tensed up at that, so I said, "I'm at peace knowing I've got you forever now, but that just makes me feel worse for Bev."

Lucy propped herself up on her elbow and looked down at me, cricking her mouth to the side like she did when she wasn't quite sure about something. "Let's give her some time," she finally said. "Then we'll try to get you a visitor's pass to Before." She slid out of bed and put on her robe. "I have to be honest, though: I don't think you'll qualify for a pass. She's a strong woman. I doubt you'll be able to prove she needs meddling."

I swallowed my pain (and my pride at that last comment) and sat up. "Well, who do I talk to? Where do I go for the pass?"

She yanked her hair into a ponytail and glared at me. "I really don't think you should worry about *her*." She marched into the bathroom, and then I heard water running in the sink. "Anyway, it's time to get up," she yelled through the doorway. "We're meeting someone special for brunch."

I was confused for a second, because it had been a Wednesday when she shot me, and I wondered for just a moment where we'd be going for brunch on a Thursday, and then I remembered we were in the Now, and wondered for another moment if maybe every day was a weekend in the Now. And then my heart did a little flip, and I smiled. I'm a little slow, but just then it hit me, everything Lucille had told me about life and death and being with everyone you'd ever really cared about in the Now.

I ignored the screaming muscles in my chest and got out of bed. I shuffled toward the bathroom and waited until Lucy was done washing her face. "Beverly?" I asked. "Is that who we're going to see?"

Lucille whipped a hand towel off the rack and spun around. "No, we're not going to brunch with *her*," she said, blotting her scowl dry. "We're going to pick up my mother."

I must have looked pretty miserable just then, because her expression softened. "But... Bev did come around here looking for you a bit earlier." She sighed and twisted her lips. "I guess we could swing by her place after brunch."

I don't know if I could ever explain how it felt when my heart made that shift, when it had to grow big enough to contain both my joy over Beverly and the love I felt for Lucille just then. I took Lucy up in my arms and squeezed her just like I used to, so tight she could barely breathe.

And she followed through. After I discovered over brunch that I didn't really mind my Now-mother-in-law all that much, Lucy took me on over to Beverly's. Bev didn't have her Mustang—no need for cars in the Now—but I still felt that motor running when I saw her again.

Several months on, Before-Bev seems to be getting along well enough—Lucy lets me use her pass to peek in on the other side every now and then. While I feel for

Before-Bev, I never applied for a pass of my own. I don't want to meddle, because Now-Bev and I are happy, and I don't want to do anything to mess that up. And despite how I got here, I'm still on good terms with Lucille. I still want to be with her as much as I want to be with Bev. I'll always love them both.

I don't ask Lucy who she's with when we're not together, and she's stopped asking me. And I really do like it here; everything's working out fine. Except—well, sometimes I wonder how miserable Now-me actually was with the way Before-me was doing things. Could Before-me really have screwed things up that bad? And then I look at Lucy and, as much as I love her, I have to wonder if death really does change a person all that much.

New Growth

Misty watched Joe pace the living room. Things had been going missing—car keys, loose change, magazines, and now his cigarettes.

"That's the second pack this week," he growled, lifting a stack of papers off the coffee table.

"Sorry, Joe," she said from the couch.

"How does this keep happening?" He stomped into the kitchen, and Misty heard drawers opening and banging shut. The edge in his voice told her to stay on the couch, out of his way.

He stalked out of the kitchen and stood in the living room, fists on hips. Misty watched him take a deep breath in and out as he scanned shelves and windowsills. She supposed he was counting to ten. "Guess I need to get another pack," he grumbled.

She had to get him out of this mood. "Maybe Chelsea's swiping them," she said, petting the small, rust-colored tabby curled up next to her. "Maybe kitty doesn't like smoking in the house." Chelsea purred and rolled over to expose her soft white belly. Misty looked up at Joe with a tentative smile.

"The cat, eh?" His face was unreadable. Behind her smile, Misty clenched her teeth as he sat down next to her on the couch.

✦ ✦

"Babe," he said, "all you have to do is ask. I'll open a window." Misty tried not to flinch as he reached over her to give Chelsea's stomach a quick scratch. "But cigarettes aren't cheap. Where are they?"

"Joe, I'm telling you, I don't know."

Joe's eyes burned into hers for a moment before he sank back into the couch. Misty followed his gaze up to the leafy canopy hanging from the ceiling, her houseplant's silent march above their heads. Eugene, her philodendron, was thriving in his new/old home.

She'd brought Chelsea and Eugene with her when she'd moved back in with Joe. Eugene was in a bigger pot now, so the only place sturdy enough for him was on top of the squat laminate bookshelf in the corner. To keep his vines from spilling over in front of Joe's books, she'd started taping them to the walls. Since then, Eugene's tendrils had shot up to the ceiling and started to make their way across the room. She was going through tape like crazy to keep his vines from falling in Joe's way.

Misty jumped as Joe sat up with a jolt. He got down on his hands and knees to look under the couch.

"There they are!"

He pulled two packs of Lucky Strikes out from underneath the sofa and dusted them off. "Look, you don't have to hide them, I'll just open the window." He shook out a cigarette and stuck it in his mouth before patting all of his pockets.

"Now the lighter? Be back in a few," he muttered.

The front door slammed and one of Eugene's vines fell.

"I didn't hide anything," said Misty softly. She got up and pulled out a chair to stand on. The chair wobbled slightly as she looped the green, fleshy vine over her finger and tore off a length of clear tape, gently sticking the ends to the ceiling on either side of the stem. Hooks would have worked better, but Joe didn't want her putting any holes in the walls; and anyway, she liked the illusion that the vines were clinging to the ceiling on their own. All she had to do was look up, and she was in an exotic jungle far away.

She'd had Eugene even longer than she'd had Chelsea. The three of them had been through a lot over the years; moving in with—and away from—Joe, then Jeff, then Marcus, and now back with Joe. Each time she'd learned to read the signs a little bit better, to get out before the first punch was thrown. She wasn't going to take that anymore. Joe had promised, and he was trying, she could tell.

She stroked one of Eugene's large, heart-shaped leaves. She'd bought him at a flea market the first time she'd moved in with Joe, and he'd grown so fast she felt he deserved a name. She'd gone back to get another one for her mother's birthday, but the plant guy wasn't there anymore. She never came across another plant with the same leaves: light green, darker on the edges, with a purplish-red tinge down the center line.

And every time she thought about taking a clipping for her mother, the scissors were missing.

~ ~ ~

Misty came home from working the breakfast shift to find Chelsea crouching on the back of the sofa, sniffing at the fall air coming through a side window. The cat's ears twitched at the horns, sirens, and laughter drifting up from the street.

"Joe, did you leave the window open?" She shooed Chelsea away from the window and cranked the handle to close it. "Joe?"

She put her purse down on the coffee table and went back to the bedroom. The air was humid and smelled like soap, and Joe was rubbing his hair dry with a towel.

"Joe, did you leave the window open?" she asked.

"No, why?"

"Well, it was open when I got home. Chelsea was sitting right by it."

"You must have left it open yesterday." He finished drying his hair and dropped the towel onto the bed.

"No, it wasn't open this morning."

He pulled a T-shirt over his head. "Well, we should leave 'em open anyway, get some fresh air."

"Sure, but not that one, okay?" She moved past him to pick up the towel. "There's no screen; Chelsea could get out."

He looked squarely at her. "I didn't open it."

She recognized that look; that tone. She should stop pushing and just keep a better eye on Chelsea. He was trying.

The faint ringing of her phone out in the living room turned both their heads.

"Go get it," said Joe.

She squeezed by him and hurried out of the bedroom to pick it up. "Hello? Hi, Mom. No, everything's fine…"

Home at last, thought Misty, putting her key into the apartment door. This day had been a nightmare from beginning to end. She could hardly wait to vent, tell Joe how everything had conspired against her: she couldn't find her phone that morning, one of the cooks was sick, then she burned her finger trying to help out in the kitchen, then they got slammed with a tour group. And her boss was giving her that creepy look again—although she'd better leave that last part out; Joe didn't like hearing about her pervy boss.

"Joe?" she called out, throwing her keys down next to his in the bowl by the door.

"Joe?" He was there, she could feel it, but he wasn't answering. No TV, no radio—the silence was unnerving. Misty took a deep breath, chiding herself for being afraid of a little peace and quiet.

"Joe?" Passing through the tiny hallway from the door to the living room seemed to take an eternity. Joe was sitting on the couch, wearing his coat, a can of beer in his hand.

He didn't even look at her when he asked, "Where have you been?"

The quiet rage in his voice paralyzed her.

"I said, where were you?" He cocked his head and looked at her with narrowed eyes. "I've been trying to call you all day."

"I—" Misty clutched her pursestrap and tried to swallow the tremor in her voice. "I lost my phone."

Joe spoke slowly, his anger simmering in the space between each word. "Where have you been?"

"I was at work, where do you—"

"I've been trying to call you," he said, putting the can down with care.

Misty's head began to feel light. "I just told you, I lost my phone."

"Right, lost your phone," he said, rising from the couch. "You think I don't know about you and your boss?"

"What?" This had to be a bad dream.

Joe crossed over to her, his face flushed. "You too busy 'serving' your boss to pick up the phone?" His breath was hot and sour.

Misty shook her head. He said it would be different this time. "Joe, I don't know what you're—"

"Too busy to take a call from me?" he pressed. He never slurred, no matter how much he'd had to drink. "The one who's feeding you and keeping a roof over your head?"

"Joe, I'm telling you, I—"

"Oh, right, you lost your phone," he said, stepping back and throwing his hands up theatrically. "Well, let's just see, shall we? Why don't I call you right now? Let's see what happens?"

He dug his phone out of his pocket and stabbed at it with clumsy fingers, looking expectantly at the purse still dangling from her hand. She couldn't help but look down at her purse too. But the ringing came from somewhere else.

The ringing came from somewhere else, and her heart exploded with relief. Joe stood dumbly, rooted to one spot as Misty darted around the room. She followed the ringing to the bookshelf where Eugene's pot sat, then dove her hand past a curtain of lush, green leaves and pulled out the phone. The ringing stopped.

Misty turned back to Joe tentatively. He was looking at the ground. What was he thinking?

With a whisper of leaves, the tip of one of Eugene's vines plopped down on Joe's head. They both jumped. Misty put a hand to her mouth to suppress a giggle. They would both laugh about this later, she knew.

Joe looked up at the ceiling, his face wrinkled in a sneer. He reached up, hateful and quick, and tore down the vine before storming out of the room. Misty heard him claw his keys out of the bowl and slam the door behind him.

Misty stared at Eugene's broken limb on the floor. It took a moment for her to snap out of her shock and pick it up. She hurried the vine into the kitchen and filled a glass of water.

"Don't worry baby," she breathed, plunking the broken end into the water. "I'll get another pot, and some dirt, and you'll be fine. He had no right to do that to you. He can't touch any of my babies like that!"

Her breath caught.

"Where's Chelsea?" The cat always came to her as soon as she got home.

She ran back into the living room. The window was wide open.

Chelsea was gone. And she didn't dare blame Joe.

❧ ❧

Misty e-mailed all of her friends and posted a picture of Chelsea online with a plea to help find her. All week, when she wasn't at work, she searched the neighborhood for the cat, papering every open surface with Xeroxed signs. Day after day she returned to the apartment exhausted and cat-less.

She wondered if Chelsea was still alive, what she was eating, where she was sleeping. Joe wasn't much of a help with the search, but at least he'd apologized about the phone—and, when pressed, about Eugene. He was still trying, she supposed. If he could just stop drinking, at least cut down, things would get better. And as soon as she found Chelsea, everything would be whole again, she was sure of it.

"Poor Eugene," she said, stroking one of his velvety leaves. "I know you miss her too. Don't worry, I'll find her. We'll all be back together." But what kind of mother was she, letting their little family get broken up like this?

With a pang of guilt, she reached for Eugene's fertilizer. She opened the bottle and breathed in the murky odor of seaweed and rotting fish. She used to hold her breath when she fertilized Eugene, but over time she'd actually grown to like the smell. It made her feel like a good mother, giving him his special milk, rich with the nutrients he needed. She'd even tasted it once, had tried a drop of it on the tip of her tongue. It was filmy and gritty, and its sourness had turned the corners of her mouth down. She was happy to leave it all for Eugene.

She lifted the mass of vines and leaves around the edge of the pot and dribbled some of the soupy, black-brown fluid onto the dirt. She was supposed to mix it with water, but if she drank her scotch neat, she didn't see why Eugene had to settle for watered-down fertilizer. Not that she was supposed to drink scotch anymore, or anything. She had her license back and hardly ever drank anymore. She just wished Joe would cut down too.

She put the fertilizer away, turned on the TV, and lay down on the couch. Just for a few minutes…

She dreamt she was wandering in a bright, green field with Chelsea. It was a sunny day, with a slight breeze lifting her hair and playing at the gauzy white fabric of her dress. She smiled as Chelsea stalked imaginary prey in the thigh-high grass.

As she walked, clouds began to form on the horizon and the air thickened with humidity. She was amazed at how quickly the wind picked up and the sky darkened. With the wind came the sound of rustling leaves—but where were the trees? There was no shelter at all that she could see. When thunder started to rumble, she scooped Chelsea up, picked a direction, and ran, head down against the wind.

She looked up to get her bearings and saw that the clouds had turned into giant heart-shaped leaves. They were just like Eugene's, light green in the middle, dark on the edges, purplish-red down the crease. The leaves grew and multiplied, filling the sky and plunging the field into dusk. She had no idea where she was going, but ran even faster. The wind howled, and the rustling of leaves filled her ears. She looked up into the sky. All the stripes in the leaves had turned from purple to blood red.

Misty woke up with a start. The rustling in her ears stopped a moment later. She was staring straight into one of Eugene's vines, which had slipped down from the ceiling and was hanging in front of her face. She brushed it aside and sat up to see why her phone was beeping.

Joe had just texted her. He was going out with the guys—would be home a little late.

Misty bit her lip. She typed out a reply: "You the designated driver?"

But she didn't hit send. She pressed and held down the delete button and watched the words disappear one letter at a time. But he'd be suspicious if she didn't answer at all, so she sent him a simple "Ok" to keep the peace.

Misty took in a deep breath. There was still a hint of Eugene's fertilizer in the air. She went into the kitchen. Joe had a bottle of rye in there somewhere.

The rent was due. Joe was gone, and her own measly paycheck wouldn't cut it, and she didn't know what to do. It was Joe's apartment, but the manager had let her stay. He felt real bad about what had happened to Joe.

She'd woken up that night to a shout and the sounds of breaking tree limbs. She'd heard something soft and heavy hitting the pavement outside. She didn't like to remember the sound.

The police had come and gone, had interrogated her, her neighbors, his friends. He'd been drinking, they said. It looked like a very unfortunate accident, they'd told her, but don't go anywhere for the next few weeks, they may need to speak with her again.

Where would she go, anyway?

Joe's family had taken care of the arrangements, coming to town and leaving within a matter of days. She was grateful for their help. She didn't have the money for a funeral. She didn't have the money for rent. She'd been off work since the accident, sitting at home with Eugene and Chelsea. That was the one small consolation: the cat had come home again.

But how could she just go back to the restaurant like everything was normal? Nothing was normal after that night; nothing, not even her dreams. She spent her days in a stupor and her nights jerking awake every few minutes. That terrible night, and every night since, she dreamt she was Joe, coming home from the bar in the middle of the night.

She opened the front door as quietly as she could. Someone had left a light on for her. She went to turn it off and she froze, startled by the sight of twin discs glowing in the darkness outside. The cat! It was sitting on a branch just outside the window.

She reached out toward the cat. "Psst psst psst, here kitty."

Chelsea didn't move.

"Dammit, come on!" She wiggled her fingers and made kissing sounds.

Chelsea inched farther back into the tree.

Misty leaned farther out of the window. The rustling of leaves filled the room.

Misty always woke up right at this moment, trying to remember the last fragments of the dream: the lurch forward and what, aside from fear, she'd felt prickling the back of her neck before the fall.

She knew the police weren't finished with her. It would only be a matter of time before they would start asking her about Marcus. And Jeff. There had been other accidents, but never lethal—until now. How many coincidences would they be willing to believe? She was starting not to believe it herself.

Chelsea meowed from atop the dining room table. "Chelsea, what's gotten in to you?" scolded Misty, heading over to shoo her away. As the cat leapt from the table, a pair of scissors slid off and clattered on the floor.

Misty bent down and picked up the scissors. The cat meowed again.

Misty looked up at Eugene. He'd gotten huge. It would take hours for someone to unstick and untangle his vines; and even then, he'd be too big to carry with all of his new growth. If someone had to move quick and travel light…

Chelsea purred.

Misty trembled and began to cut Eugene with hands that no longer felt like her own.

Aftermilk

I. Toast

You've got to get to the toaster as soon as it pops, kids. That's the only way to butter the toast soon enough. That's your golden hour for butter, you know, when you can get it on there and spread it out like a tasty blanket of goodness, even straight from the fridge if you forgot to set it out sooner, which you usually do. There's just too much going on sometimes, you know, making sure everyone did their homework and put on pants and found their shoes and the eggs aren't burning, and then you look up and the toaster's popped long ago and already cooling, and you've missed your window. I'm not blaming you, kids; that's just how it is sometimes, too much to pay attention to at once.

But kids, on those days when you don't miss your window and you get there in time, you can do magic. That butter goes on the toast quiet as a cat's paws on carpet, and it soaks right in like rain on the beach, and the bread gets as soft as it was the moment it was born, like right when it came out of the oven, and that's when it smelled the best, too, so it's almost like going back and getting a second chance. And then you bite into it, because when you've buttered it like that, who needs jam, and the butter seeps out on your tongue, sweet and salty and warm, and it's better than anything you've had in your mouth for years.

I'm just saying it's a real shame when you miss that window, kids.

You miss that window, the best you can hope for is that you remembered to put your butter out soon enough, so it can warm up a little. And maybe you even put it close to the toaster for a little melty action, because you found out the hard way the microwave was too much. That's what you call the nuclear option, like that biker Mommy dated after the divorce.

You kids wouldn't remember him. You mostly stayed with your father then.

So no butter dish in the microwave, okay? If you miss the toaster window, you'll just have to scrape little pieces off your stick of butter and dot your slice with them, and if you hurry, your toast will only be dry in patches. And if you don't think about the way it could have flowed like honey had you got there quicker, you won't miss it too much when it doesn't taste as sweet.

Doesn't pay to think too much on the past, kids. Don't cry over spilled milk or cold toast. You just buck up and make do when you miss your window, even if you forget to take the butter out of the fridge first. Then you just grit your teeth and scrape off as thin a sheet of butter as you can, like a surgeon, and transfer that slice to your cold crunchy toast, which is probably even a little burned because you bumped the dial when you moved the toaster out of the puddle of juice someone spilled—and left on the counter, mind you, like he didn't have hands to clean it up himself—anyway, you moved the toaster out of the juice so you wouldn't electrocute yourself, and then put the plate on top of the toaster for maybe a hint of warmth, because you know—again, from experience—that you can't even put the whole thing in the microwave, toast and all, and use the toast as a butter buffer, because then the bread will get all chewy and stale, just like your second go-around with that biker who was already too much the first time. (Learn from your mistakes, kids, that's all Mommy asks.)

So you go ahead and drag that little sheet of butter across dry land, knife screeching like it's raking a chalkboard, until the butter breaks into smaller shards, and you shove that rubble across the desert until it rubs down to pebbles, which you finally have to cram into the toast, which you've fractured and flattened by now, so it looks like one of those videos of water frozen into shelves of ice at the shore. Then you think about all the shredded toast you've had to choke down already, and how many more greasy slices of sawdust you'll have to choke down in the years to come, now that it's too late to go back and spread manna on warm, lightly crisp, sweet-smelling bread.

But you can't torture yourself, thinking back to those days when you used to catch it just in time, all the time, when it was just you and your radio and your tea, and maybe later you'd head to the market or a café with a friend before your date with the cute law student that night—he was taking you to dinner somewhere you never could have paid for yourself, and frankly neither could he, not at the moment, but both of you knew it would just be a matter of time till he became partner, in more ways than one, or so you thought before everything else happened and you wound up with the other boy who would become your ex—and you weren't worried about a thing because you thought you had all the time in the world.

But look at that kids, toast is done. Here's the butter, hurry up. That's it, see that butter glide? Hear those cat's paws on carpet? Smell that bakery? Quickly now, get it all the way to the edges. Hurry up, before it dries out. Things have a way of crumbling apart when you wait too long.

II. Love and orange juice

Never get the orange juice with pulp, kids. It's disgusting. If you want pulp, eat an orange. That's the whole point of orange juice, to have just the juice. Don't ever trust a drink you have to chew. Except for Blizzards.

No, we're not going to Dairy Queen for breakfast. Mommy has some standards, no matter what Daddy might say. I know he makes you drink orange juice with pulp when you're at his house. He always knew how much I hated that stuff, but he still kept on buying it. He said I was just being picky, said it was silly to buy more than one kind of OJ and fill up the fridge with doubles. He'd come back from the store with a huge family size jug of it, to save money, he said, but really it was just because he was… Forget it. I know he asks you kids what I say about him.

Anyway, he tried to get me to drink it with pulp, saying it was healthier, like how all the vitamins from vegetables were in the peel, but I'd just use my fork and lift all those nasty sacs out of there until it was drinkable.

Drove him crazy. Even when we had both in the fridge, sometimes I'd be running late and not exactly looking, and I'd pour myself half a glass of that pulped-up sludge before I realized what I was doing, and he always got bent out of shape if I asked him to drink it for me, cause he'd already had his by then and said he'd be pissing orange with all the extra juice I made him drink. So I said fine, I'd pour it out and that about made him blow his top. "Prodigal" was his word. What does that mean? It means a person who doesn't want to chew on a glass full of slimy juice bags.

You don't mind it? Well, that's nice of you, trying not to hurt Daddy's feelings like that. You kids always were kind, you got that from me. Like when he forgot things, which he always did, I didn't always rub his nose in it, you know. In fact, I even told him why I hate OJ with pulp, told him more than once, but he never seemed to remember it when he hit the juice aisle in the grocery store and came home with a carton of nightmares. Well, "nightmares" is a bit strong, but definitely bad memories. Because here's the lesson, kids, always eat breakfast before you start in on the screwdrivers.

It's a drink, kids. Mommy wasn't always as smart as she is now. I made some questionable decisions when I was young, and it's your job to learn from them. See, there was a tradition at high school—you've got a long way to go before then, kids, but you should still hear this. This tradition was called Senior Skip Day. It was in the spring, when the teachers were still teaching, but the kids were just about full up on learning. It was always the second Friday in May, so everyone knew when it was, even the kids who weren't seniors yet. Well, one year, when I was one of those underclassmen, a friend and I decided to join in on Senior Skip Day—but we didn't know where any parties were or anything, so it just turned out to be Two Sophomore Girls Skip Day. So we went over to another girl's house, and turns out she had a party right there under her bed in the form of a fifth of Smirnoff. That's vodka, kids, a nasty, nasty kind of alcohol that looks like water but is anything but.

Long story short, kids, we got those screwdrivers wrong that morning. A real screwdriver is vodka plus probably more orange juice than we were using, plus not on an empty stomach at ten in the morning. We got it all wrong, and as a consequence, Mommy got sick, real sick, and it turns out that orange pulp is not so easy to wipe from the floors or from the memory. So ever since then, orange juice with pulp is not how Mommy wants to start her day. And Daddy knows that, because I've told him more than once, and really, why was pulp more important to him than making his wife happy?

Anyway, don't tell him I said that, kids, he'll just get upset. But let this be a lesson to you, and it's not just about orange juice. Whatever your pulp is in life, be it ambition or religion or where to live or how many kids to have, or whether to have them at all, never stay with someone who doesn't respect your feelings about it. Not that they have to give in, but if you can't even have equal cartons in the fridge, kids, it's time to pack your bags and go somewhere you can have your own fridge for a change, your own fridge with your own stuff you put there with your own hard work. Because you've always been able to do it, you just didn't know it because you'd always been told you'd never be able to do it on your own.

Don't ever fall for that line, kids. You deserve something out of life, and you can accomplish anything you put your minds to. And you should never be ashamed of following your own goals, large or small. Even if it's something as simple as sitting at your own table in the morning quiet and sipping on a nice, cool glass of orange juice without pulp.

III. Aftermilk

Kids, I've eaten way too many bowls of slush in my life, and I don't want the same for you. So listen: don't walk away from your cereal once you've poured the milk. Just don't.

You may think you can have it all, wrinkle-free laundry from the dryer *and* a delicious bowl of Mini-Wheats, but that's an illusion. You hear that buzzer, you block it out, or you'll be walking back to a bowl of pablum with jagged icebergs of wheat sticking up as if they'd tried to claw their way out of the brew.

And don't open the mail after you pour, kids. Don't even look at the mail. Because let me tell you, one phone call about an erroneous charge on your credit card and you'll come back to a swamp full of slimy, bloated Kix corpses you'll have to shovel into your squawker one spoonful after another. It doesn't help that they were stale to begin with. Family size may be cheaper, but it's a heavy price to pay when it's just you and your roommate.

Yes, this was before I met Daddy, before I had you two.

Of course you always have to eat it. It's not like you have money to burn, like you can just throw that nasty goop down the disposal. It's not like you can buy the actual brand names, either. Mommy didn't always have Post and Kellogg's in her house, kids. The stars of her shelves were Kroger and Freddys, or whatever chain store happened to be on her bus line.

Yes, kids, it's nice that we can have Lucky Charms now. So why aren't you eating them? Milk's poured, clock's ticking, school bus is on the way. Didn't you hear a word I said?

You learn early to avoid the puffs and the flakes. You learn soon enough to stick with the clusters, the granolas. They might just have a little crunch left by the time you're done holding your roommate's hair back while she throws up—morning sickness, and you knew that bastard Randy was gonna cut bait as soon as he caught wind of it, and she'd have to move back in with her parents, and you'd have to find another roommate, and sure enough, that's exactly what happened. So always use a condom, kids, and stick with your clusters and granolas.

And know that even Grape-Nuts are no match for certain phone calls. Because sometimes that phone rings, and you think you're just going to pick up for a quick chat with your boyfriend, and by the time you hang up, you've got no more boyfriend because he doesn't believe you when you swear you haven't been sneaking money out of his wallet, when all you had to do was ask. And maybe he's right because you've been pretending you can afford real Grape-Nuts, and genuine Cheerios and actual Special K, and all just to make him think you had it together enough to buy name brands, but all you have left now is a heaping portion of room temperature fiber stew.

No, kids, that wasn't Daddy. That was before Mommy met Daddy. But let that be a lesson to you, it doesn't pay to lie. It's not nice to lie, even though everyone does it sometimes. Sometimes you have to, like when you plan a surprise party and you can't tell the person before it happens. Or when you two ask what you're going to get for your birthdays and I say, "I don't know." You don't *really* want to know, do you?

I didn't think so. See, sometimes people tell little lies to make other people feel better. Remember when your friend Tina got that crazy haircut, but you both told her it looked good so she wouldn't feel bad? You said the other kids teased her, but you two were nice to her even though you don't really like her.

Those types of lies aren't really lies, they're more like *kindnesses*. Like, it's a kindness when your parents say school simply wasn't the place where you could show your best strengths, or when your friends say sure, you could be a star, you just have to want it bad enough. It's a kindness when agent after agent tells you they'd love to sign you, but producers wouldn't know what to do with your kind of beauty. It's a kindness when your friends say how inspiring it is that you keep chasing your dreams, despite everything. It's a kindness when the guy you're dating, a regular where you waitress, asks you to marry him shortly after the condom breaks, says he was going to ask you anyway. And it's a kindness when you say yes. But then you think maybe kindnesses aren't always that great after all, because somehow all those kindnesses led to a bunch of meanness, and now Mommy and Daddy don't live together anymore.

But kids, don't misunderstand me: all that kindness, and even the meanness, was all worth it in the end, because look what Mommy got out of it. I got you! I could never have imagined finding something as beautiful as you two on my path of little white lies. And that's not just another kindness, kids. I really mean it.

Listen. Hear the clock chiming? You've got ten minutes to finish up and catch the school bus. Go learn something. Pay attention to Teacher like your lives depend on it. And remember, no failsafe is safe from failure, but even if you mess up, you can still salvage something beautiful out of life.

But first, finish your cereal, kids. Go on. Eat every last spoonful before it all turns to mush.

Another Damn Cottage

It was another damn cottage, another damn grand-mother, frail and helpless, waiting for a handout sent via grandchild. The wolf knocked, ate the grandmother, choking down her stringy, slightly rank flesh. He left a leg, not wanting to fill his belly up. He wanted the soft, fatty flesh of a child to top it off, that plump taste lingering on his tongue. He looked out the window, saw a flash of red in the forest, licked his lips.

It was another damn wolf, another damn axe, heavy and rusty. Red grabbed the weathered handle and levered it out of the tree stump in front of the cottage. She sucked in a breath and jammed her thumb into her mouth, new splinter stinging. Another wolf pelt, another mess to clean up, another dead grandmother. But this time, at least, something left over to bury.

It was another bungled case, another damn vigilante stealing the show. The knight threw down his sword as Red shuffled out of the cottage, a granny's withered leg slung over her shoulder, deepening the red of her cloak. The knight's chin quivered, and he dropped to his knees, holding his hands out toward the poor child. She stumbled over to him and slid the weight off her shoulder into his arms.

"Take this over to the Andersens, would you?" She patted the leg. "Tell them I'm sorry I didn't get here in time."

The knight stared slack-jawed at the puckered limb, then back up at Red.

"I'd do it myself," she said, "but I've got another call. And this time, I can't be late."

Red tightened the string of her cloak and ran off into the forest. Another damn cottage, another damn grandmother, and ever since losing both of her own, always another damn thing to prove.

With thanks to Joyce Carol Oates and Little Red Riding Hood

Bedpea

The sky was slate; the trees were naked. The hag screeched from the peak of the pyre, bound to the stake, ropes thick enough to hold until the end. A blast of chill wind carried her shrieks out over the crowd. She would soon be warm enough. Once our revered queen, she would become another victory in our war against the Evil One. And I, behind my mask, would light the cleansing pyre.

From time to time the sibyl stopped her screaming. Still, the Dark Lord did not leave her: she strained against the ropes, smashing the back of her head against the post, teeth clenched and bared like a wolverine's until, exhausted, she slackened, shivering in her burlap shift, hair cloaking her face like a shredded gray curtain.

The pious villagers surrounding the platform murmured, ate celebratory cheese and bread, eyed the brazier expectantly. At the magistrate's signal, I would tip my torch through the grate, ignite it, and excise this evil from our kingdom.

I'd heard the tale—the visitor in the storm, claiming to be a princess. The king's interest, he said, in a suitable bride for the prince. The queen, suspicious of this unknown girl, ordered the test: a pea under twenty mattresses and twenty eider-down beds. The next morning, bruises on pale young flesh. And blood.

Witchcraft was the only explanation.

The crone rolled her head toward me, staring down under heavy lids from atop the kindling. I never looked the condemned in the eye—and yet, she'd been my queen. Her lips moved. I leaned closer. I barely heard her above the restless buzz: "Please, good sir, release me. The verdict is untrue."

But I was just the executioner.

A cheer rose from the crowd. The magistrate climbed the steps and stood by my side. He unscrolled the judgment and read it aloud to the villagers' boos and jeers. I remained still and mute, as my profession required.

"Please," she whimpered, and I could not help but look again, perhaps as the final sign of a former subject's respect.

I searched her eyes for evil. I sought the demonic spark that had invited its Dark Lord into the palace to so heinously violate the princess. I searched and searched.

The magistrate's voice rang low and clear: "Let the sentence be carried out."

I lit my torch.

The process had been fair and just, and in her survival of the trials, the wicked woman had proved herself a bride of Satan. She could not escape God's wrath.

I looked up again and hunted for the perfidy in her eyes.

"Mercy," she gasped. "I am innocent."

I turned away from her. The square was full of shining, righteous faces, tilted upward in anticipation. The king's messenger, the only one who could deliver a pardon, was nowhere to be seen.

The magistrate, again: "Let the sentence be carried out!"

I lit the pyre.

Our queen melted into moans as the bonfire licked her tattered burlap hem. She wailed for God while the flames grabbed at her shift and pulled themselves up her legs. Her hair curled and crisped; her head rolled from side to side on its weakened stalk. Between the popping of wood and the whoosh of flames rushing up her chest, it was impossible to tell when she stopped shrieking.

I followed the magistrate down the stairs and into the courthouse. I changed my clothing and exited without my mask, thus masking my way home.

And now I sit, staring into my hearth, drinking until the flames blur.

Foul black smoke will choke the square, driving away most of the crowd long before the last embers die out. A few will remain, looking for keepsakes, a fingerbone or a tooth.

Early tomorrow, when the sun pinks the sky, attendants will sweep the ashes and replenish the wood. Soon after, the first spectators will enter the square, flushed and gossiping in anticipation of a second burning so soon. Both for witchcraft, they will prattle. And both royalty.

I marvel at the confluence of so much evil in our kingdom. The princess, an innocent visitor, so grievously harmed within palace walls. This should have made her an object of pity. But the Evil One is insidious, defiling the poor maiden not once, but evermore, infusing her mind with vile, impossible thoughts. In seeking to explain her violation, she only revealed the depth of her despoilment—for only the Brazen One would make such accusations about our king.

So spoke the magistrate.

And I am just the executioner.

Tomorrow I will seek the Devil in the eyes of a princess. I do not fear the evil I might see there. I fear its absence. Again.

You, Commuter

We see you waiting at a bus stop, trying to get to work. Busses idle in a row at the curb. Dozens of people fume in the drizzle, but all the doors are closed, and nothing is moving.

One man pounds at a door, harder and harder. He almost disables the bus prying it open. You follow the grumbling crowd aboard. You're irate, and you make sure your feet stomp on the stairs.

We turn the wheel with the driver, and as you ride into the city you realize you have no idea whether you're on the right bus. We watch you in the mirror. You're looking out the window. You're going east, and you were supposed to be going north.

You also realize you've forgotten to put on clothing, beyond your bra, underwear, and raincoat. You button up over goosepimpling skin, track landmarks out the window, and plot the fastest way home.

While we pace the aisle, you glance down at your legs and find they are covered in black denim. You open your coat just enough to spot a sliver of blue silk. You exhale and look back out at the rain-slicked streets. One more stop and you can transfer. You calculate: home, change, back to work. Minutes will add up to hours.

We slump into the seat behind you. You look down: you're wearing a white T-shirt. You wonder if your clothes will change every time you look at them. Will you wind up naked? You try to stare out the window, but your eyes trip on a glimpse of red wool.

You picture your deadlines crashing like hometown mailboxes on Halloween. We lean forward, sniff your shampoo. Flowers. There's no time for home. Keep going. Just don't look down.

We don't know when you can look down again.

Speculum Crede

Marie hadn't been looking forward to the company picnic that year, even before her daughter began to turn green. But until her little Lisa shrank and sprouted a stem and turned into a hopping green bean, it had all merely been an annoyance: making enough potato salad to fill her jumbo yellow casserole dish, packing Bobby Jr. into his car seat, and pulling grown Bobby, her husband, away from his ESPN to steer their Caravan to Mirror Pond Park.

Before Lisa turned into a green bean and Bobby Jr. turned into a honeypot, and she turned… Before any of that happened, she was simply annoyed at having to spend Saturday in work mode. As the Caravan pulled in to the picnic parking lot, and pre-bean Lisa shot out and ran for the food, and she lifted Bobby Jr. out of his car seat and onto her hip, and pulled her shirt down over her out-of-shape belly and headed toward her coworkers, Bobby and casserole in tow, the only thing on her mind was how long they had to stay to be polite.

There they all were, her coworkers: Denise from Sales, Roger from Accounting, the guy from IT who was content to go simply by "I.T." because those were his initials and his whole name was exotic and unpronounceable. And there was the CEO, Lavinia Hart, and her minion Ansel Evans, the two "overlords" standing off to the side, staring at their employees as though examining a bad rash.

Marie noted the CEO's stylish blue dress. She let go of her husband's hand and tugged down on her shirt again.

"Mommy, can I go get a plate?" asked Lisa.

And that's when it started.

Marie looked down at her daughter. She could have sworn something green flashed in the girl's eyes.

"Sweetpea?" she asked, kneeling in front of Lisa. "You feeling all right?"

The edges of the girl's pupils seemed to waver. A green tinge seeped out from the twin black spots, staining her once brown irises and tinting the whites of her eyes. Marie froze as Lisa's face and body turned the color of grass. The girl grew greener and greener, and her body started to bend and shrink.

Now she had one more reason to boycott all future company picnics.

Lavinia Hart, President and CEO of Haverton Industries, stood just outside the covered picnic area with a bottle of Perrier, watching her employees enter with their pots and bowls and casseroles. For form's sake, she'd have to partake. But she'd have to run twice as long the next few days to burn through all the butter and cream and pasta bedecking the table.

She scowled at an awkward-looking man, IT no doubt, adding a bag of chips to the "bounty."

The sodium, she thought, tapping her mauve nails against the green glass bottle. She patted at her auburn hair, swept up into a purposely down-to-earth ponytail for the outdoors, then brushed invisible dirt off her sleeveless blue silk dress.

"Mr. Evans," she said, summoning her Director of HR with the flick of a bejeweled finger.

A caramel-colored man wearing creased khaki shorts stepped closer. "Yes, Ms. Hart?"

"Next year, we're having this catered."

"But Ms. Hart, you said—"

The sun glinted off her Cartier watch as she raised a hand to silence him. "I work hard enough to provide jobs for these people. There are limits to what I can be asked to endure."

Ansel Evans ran a quick calculation in his head. There was nowhere left to cut. Travel had been curtailed, employee bonuses eliminated, raises frozen—the potluck picnic was their last ditch effort to keep the workers marginally happy. Yet the shareholders still wanted more blood from the stone. One by one, all but the legally required employee benefits would go on the chopping block—and then the employees themselves.

Or, they could try again to revisit executive compensation.

He stole a glance at Lavinia. She was glaring at a steaming bowl of white something-or-other dotted with red god-knows-what on the picnic table. Maybe he could use this moment, her revulsion, to redirect the company budget a bit. If she didn't want to be forced to choke down KFC and mystery salad at these events, perhaps she could think about an adjustment in her own benefits package. It would at least be a goodwill gesture for the employees.

"Yes, Mr. Evans?"

He suppressed a jump. He'd been too busy formulating his argument in his head to notice her staring. He wondered how a being with such cold eyes could withstand sunlight.

What was going on inside that head? First she'd suggested doing away with staff parties altogether, and now she wanted them catered? The only constant with her was that whatever she decided, he would be the face of doom. As Director of HR, he was the messenger of every policy he tried to advise her against.

"Mr. Evans, what is it?"

Her eyes glinted at him from the armor of her perfect makeup, one eyebrow slightly cocked, lips curved in an almost imperceptible smile.

"Nothing, Ms. Hart."

That's the way it was: Marketing made all the exciting announcements to the world, he delivered the sucker-punches to the employees.

As if Marie didn't have enough to deal with, with her daughter turning green, Bobby Jr. started to change at the same time. He grew rounder and cooler in Marie's arms and—sticky. Marie gave a little yelp and almost dropped him. She clutched him harder as he took on the shape of a bowl.

"Mommy, can we get our plates?" asked the green bean, jumping up and down where her daughter had stood. Marie squinted at it. It looked more like a peapod, actually, with a little purple flower bobbing at the end of a curly vine corkscrewing up from the top of its… head, she supposed.

She heard a growl behind her and turned to see a tall, white bear holding her casserole dish.

"You okay?" rumbled the bear. A fine, shining powder drifted from his muzzle, and between the growls, he sounded something like Bobby.

Marie nodded shakily. So she was crazy. Okay. Just don't scare the kids.

The bear cocked his glistening head to one side, then bent down toward the peapod. "Come on, let's fix a plate for you and Mommy, okay?"

With a soft scraping sound, the bear led the peapod toward the picnic tables. White powder sloughed off the bear's arms and legs, drifting toward Marie in the wind. It was light and sweet, like sugar dust. Sugar. Her Sugarbear. Walking with her Sweetpea.

She looked down at Bobby Jr. in her arms. Sure enough, she was holding a honeypot straight out of Winnie-the-Pooh, complete with "HUNNY" on the side. Even though the pot was sticky, it was suddenly hard for her to hold. Her fingers were fusing together, and she barely had enough time to set the pot down onto the grass before her hands turned into long, paddle-shaped flippers. She let out a gasp, which came out like some sound from a nature show.

"Momma, up!" burbled the honeypot.

Marie looked around. The giant white bear was chatting with her completely unfazed coworkers while loading chicken and potato salad onto paper plates. Her peapod child was jumping around on the table between pies and cakes. Bobby Jr. blurped stickily in the grass, and she looked down at herself to see taut, grey skin stretched over a stout belly. She groaned—and then recognized the sound. It was from a show they'd watched just the week before called "Masters of the Ocean." Feeling around with her pectoral fins, she confirmed that her teeth had been replaced with baleen. She took a deep breath in and out, almost fainting when water spritzed out the blowhole in back of her head.

Lavinia Hart squinted at the plump woman with a toddler at her feet. She didn't know her name, but she recognized her from infrequent forays into the bowels of Administration.

"Mr. Evans, is something wrong with that woman?"

"Which one?"

"Her," she said, pointing toward the frumpy, spaced-out-looking woman running her hands over her mouth and the back of her head. "I think she's hyperventilating. Do something."

Mr. Evans moved quickly toward the distressed woman and escorted her to a seat. Lavinia appreciated his responsiveness in all matters. As she noted in his appraisals year after year, she could always count upon him to handle any unpleasantness with employees with the utmost aplomb: the phasing out of pensions, the switch to less costly healthcare, the undetectably targeted early retirement scheme of two years ago. He had borne the brunt of all these very necessary decisions with perfect professionalism, leaving her free to chart the company's course into calmer, more profitable waters.

He is most malleable, she thought. And just then her words played a very clever little trick on her eyes, for at that moment she saw him as a giant marshmallow. A Peep, to be precise. He was a caramel-colored Peep rabbit hopping next to the odd woman, who was now a fat pink Peep bird.

At risk to her professional demeanor, Lavinia giggled at the sight, bringing a paw up to her muzzle to cover her smile.

Lavinia stopped mid-giggle—which had sounded rather like a purr, now that she thought of it—and stared down at her paws. They were large and powerful, and covered in golden brown fur. She turned them over and over again, flexing the fingers (or toes?) to test that they were, in fact, hers. A shiver prickled down her spine when she unsheathed her claws, dangerous and wonderful.

Her eyes roamed down her long, sleek body. She admired her silky fur—milky-white on her frontside, golden brown along her flanks—and marveled at her muscular legs, which ended in the same formidable paws as the ones she held in front of her.

Lavinia's tail twitched. It had finally happened! All of the management books she'd skimmed had implored her to visualize success, visualize her strength and capability and—though they did not explicitly say this, she could read it between the lines—her superiority to all those around her. She'd tried it, privately of course, so fleetingly and noncommittally no one would perceive her failure, not even herself. But now she had succeeded, and it all seemed so real!

She looked up from her beautiful body and saw that indeed, all of her employees were mere Peeps before her. A maroon Peep rabbit threw a Frisbee to a little green chick. A large, aqua Peep bird tended the grill, its beak drooping slightly over the hot coals. Blue, pink, purple, yellow, green—all possible hues of marshmallow Peep creatures hopped around the picnic tables.

Lavinia suppressed a giggly purr. This was amazing! She'd truly broken through. This was the mental edge she needed to visualize her next takeover. Franzen Enterprises, perhaps? Her ears twitched with anticipation, and she sent her paws up to stroke them. She could actually feel their velvety fur. She was unstoppable! She took a deep breath, wondering if she dared. It would be unseemly, but she couldn't contain herself: she opened her muzzle and let out a deep, throaty roar.

Ansel had an arm around Marie and was directing her toward a bench when an intense, rumbling buzz shook the earth beneath his feet. The sound came from behind, where he'd been standing with Lavinia. He let go of Marie and spun around, fully expecting to see a fallen hive explode into a swarm of angry bees.

What he saw was just one massive bee. It was a queen, six feet long, reclining on the grass with a pile of volleyball-sized eggs at its end.

"What?" it said to him.

He blinked.

"What are you staring at?" it asked, sounding like a buzzy version of Lavinia Hart. "Mr. Evans, come here please."

He had no choice but to fly toward it—her, and almost tumbled out of the air in shock at his sudden flight ability. He landed at her feet with a bump.

The queen bee twitched her antennae and let another egg slip from her rear. "What's gotten into you?"

"I—" Ansel clamped his mandibles shut at his own buzzy voice. Something fluttered behind him, and he twisted around to find new, nearly transparent wings on his back. He jumped again and gasped, wrapping yellow, multi-jointed legs around his hard, black chest. Dazed, he tapped on his exoskeleton while curling down to look at the black and yellow stripes of his firm, oval abdomen.

"Mr. Evans," buzzed Ms. Hart, "if you are not here to sting me to death, destroy my hive, and carry away my eggs to feed your young, then why are you looking at me like that?" Another glistening egg slid from her abdomen and rolled down the side of the pile into the grass.

"P—pardon?"

"I said, you don't look well. Do you have heatstroke?"

He opened his mandibles and looked away, confused and embarrassed by the birthing taking place next to the picnic tables. That woman Marie had been acting strangely too—maybe there was something in the air. An ill-timed spraying of pesticide, perhaps? Toxic pollen? He looked around for the woman with the toddler, desperate to find out if she was also having hallucinations. But he could no longer tell her apart from anyone else.

Everyone around him had become a three-foot-tall bee. They walked upright, scraping pollen off their legs into wax bowls, drinking nectar from flower-shaped cups, placing their pupae on swings and pushing them high into the air. He shuddered and hugged his slender waist.

His *slender* waist…

He was a wasp, the utmost enemy of bees—in a whole picnic full of them!

"Mr. Evans," the queen demanded, "are you not feeling well?"

He turned to face the queen. Another egg slipped free of her body. He looked down and said, "I don't believe I am, Ms. Hart. I believe I should go home."

"Then do so, and take care of yourself this weekend. We need you bright and early Monday morning."

"Yes, ma'am," said Ansel, and after an awkward glance around, he fluttered his wings and took off.

He was bewildered. It actually worked; he was flying! He flew higher and higher until all the bees at the picnic looked as small as bees should actually be. He swooped and whirled with the wind, frightened, incredulous— and exhilarated!

But he had no idea how long this hallucination would last. He had a horrible thought of turning back into himself halfway home and tumbling down through the roof of someone's house.

So, in his eminently practical way, he dove back toward his Prius and drove home.

Droplets rained down Marie's back as she released a breath through her blowhole. She felt around for a sticky spot on honeypot-Bobby Jr. and maneuvered him up from the ground into her flippers, hoping Mr. Evans had gone away. He was a little hard to track now that he'd turned into a snake. Grass grew up around him as he slithered about: thick, green blades sprouting through gravel, dirt—even asphalt—to cloak his winding form, then disappearing again as he passed. In fact, she only knew there was a snake in the roving patch of grass because he had risen out of it to help her. After a moment of abject terror, she had recognized the snake as Mr. Evans from the hollow, dutiful manner in which he had escorted her to her chair.

He'd slunk off, and she'd tried to calm down. But she was still a whale. And her husband was still a sugarbear who was upset that his wife refused to eat the plate of krill he'd brought her.

A little yellow butterfly flapped up to the family and asked Sweetpea if she wanted to play. The peapod bent in Marie's direction, and she said "Yes, baby, go ahead." Her daughter leapt up and tried to hop after the butterfly, but it flitted and floated far above her. Sweetpea stopped and bent down, then jumped as high as she could. As she jumped, she turned into a little green butterfly with purple spots on its wings. She and the yellow butterfly tumbled over one another in dizzying circles before fluttering toward a larger cloud of butterflies.

Marie's baleen crinkled as she smiled after her daughter.

Sugarbear stood up and took the honeypot from her. "Come on, little man," he said. "Let's go see what this sandbox is all about!"

As Bobby Jr. rolled around in the pit, Marie wondered how they'd get all the sand out of his sticky pot once they got home. But of course that was just an idle thought, she insisted to herself, since this was all a temporary hallucination.

Marie wondered if maybe the heat was making her see things. She rose and tiptoed precariously on the flukes of her tail to a folding chair in the shade, breathing a sigh of relief when it didn't crack under her weight. She flipped her tail up and down, waiting for everything to go back to normal; but the more she looked around, the more she realized it really wasn't that different. Sleek young stallions from Sales pranced around the HR intern, a leggy gazelle. Ornery old hens sat to the side, clucking amongst themselves about how short shorts had gotten nowadays; and the former-football-player VP of Marketing, a spiral ham, chucked a football to I.T., who looked to her like a circuit board. That last one disappointed her a bit: if she were going to have hallucinations, couldn't they at least be a little more original?

Maybe that was her problem. Maybe her ideas weren't outside-the-box enough to get promoted. Lord knows she'd applied for enough jobs higher up at Haverton. She was plenty capable, even if she wasn't the young, aggressive type Ansel and Lavinia favored. But all those times she thought she was contributing in all-staff meetings, maybe they saw just another old hen clucking from the sidelines.

The roving cloud of butterflies flitted closer to the picnic tables. Marie's little green Sweetpea tumbled to the ground, hopped up to her and asked, "Can I have something to drink, Momma?"

Before she could answer, Sugarbear hurried over with a grimy Bobby Jr. in his arms. "Hey guys, how 'bout we head home now," he said, shifting from foot to foot.

Marie squinted up at him. "You okay, Bobby?"

"Yeah, I just—" He jiggled the baby in his arm. "It's hot, I need to get out of this sun."

"But I'm thirsty," whined Lisa.

Marie pushed herself up from her chair, glad for an excuse to leave. "There's water in the car, Sweetpea. Let's go."

Bobby packed the kids off to the car while Marie rushed through goodbyes and grabbed their casserole. It was still half full, she noticed. They *were* leaving pretty early. But they weren't the only ones: as they walked out to the parking lot, she saw Lavinia Hart mount her broomstick and fly away.

Lavinia prowled about her penthouse, unsure of what to do with all her newfound energy. Since coming home from the picnic, she'd already run an easy 20 miles on her treadmill and devoured all the meat in her freezer. Meatcicles, why hadn't anyone ever thought of this before?

She licked a paw and sent it back to smooth down her fur. She shouldn't have blown it dry after her shower. Force of habit. Now she looked like she was trying to puff her hair up into a bombastic male mane. She had no need for such theatrics. Better to be the sleek huntress, the one you admired for its beauty and only realized was dangerous when its teeth were already at your throat.

If only usurping Franzen Enterprises could be that easy. But hunting down their CEO would only land her in jail, or in keeping with her visualization, the zoo.

No, she needed a real plan. Her thinking was always clearest when she was in motion, so she went down to the complex spa for a swim. With a rush of delight, she slipped into the empty pool, grateful for solitude. She swam almost until closing, relishing the sure, swift power of her legs pulling her muscular body forward in the water. She was mindful of the time, however. She pulled herself out of the water and shook her fur dry, slinking back up to her penthouse before Danny the lecherous night watchman came on duty. He sometimes took it upon himself to "patrol" the pool—for resident safety, he said. Right now she didn't want any contact with people to break her powerful trance, least of all him.

Upstairs again, she dropped to all fours and sauntered into her living room, leaving damp pawprints in her wake. Her reflection in the floor-to-ceiling windows was sleek, sharp against the darkness outside. No, she couldn't let this go to waste. She padded closer to the window, squinting through it to look at the traffic below. She rose to her hind legs, pressed her front paws against the window and purred. Her eyesight was astounding now! A taxi stopped at a red light, and she could see all the car's detailing. She could even see the passengers inside. A man looked up at her through the rear window of the cab. He turned to someone else, and both men twisted to look in her direction, finally rolling down their windows and poking their heads out.

Lavinia gasped and crossed her front paws over her chest.

Someone on the sidewalk stopped, and the men in the taxi laughed and pointed up at her window. The pedestrian looked up—and grinned.

She jumped back from the glass with a yelp. What did she look like to them? She'd been wearing her blue Dior sundress that morning, and she didn't remember taking it off. Was she a giant wet cat in a ruined dress? A sopping wet woman in clinging blue silk? Or a stark naked woman standing in front of a window at night for the whole world to see?

A low, guttural growl rattled her throat. She rushed forward and yanked the drapes closed. Shame mixed with adrenaline and morphed into rage. Vulnerability was her worst enemy—she would make it her prey. She would pounce on it and hold it down, feel it strain under her jaws. She closed her eyes and imagined herself annihilating weakness, its eyes rolling wildly as its hooves thrashed in the air.

That was just a start, she thought, growling and stalking about her living room. She would visualize herself into something even more powerful, something no man would dare to leer or laugh at. Ever again.

Ansel Evans looked into the mirror and grabbed at his head and thorax, trying to feel a human form underneath. His shower had failed to wash off his insanity. Even his mother had heard it when she'd called. "Baby, you sick?" she'd asked, fretting over his raspy voice. She'd heard it! It was real.

He flopped onto his couch with a jar of honey and a spoon. He was a wasp working in a nest of honeybees. Surely it was just a matter of time before they'd turn on him. Truth be told, he'd felt their hate brewing long before the picnic. Every layoff, every cutback, every degradation of worker's rights—the news had all been his to deliver.

He dunked the spoon into the jar and smashed a spoonful of honey against his face. He tried again, opening his mandibles as wide as they would go. It still didn't fit. With a sigh, he slumped over the dripping spoon and stuck his tongue into the honey.

All this to please Lavinia Hart. But to what end? He'd been a Director for eight years now, watching one imbecile after another get promoted to Vice President around him. Even that meathead from Marketing was a VP now. And where was *Ansel's* VP slot? Where was *his* recompense for a job well done, again and again? For all the dirty work done to prop up Lavinia Hart?

He put down the honey and stood, wings thrumming. He wasn't going to be her patsy anymore. He was going to take his rightful place.

Ansel paced back and forth in front of his couch. He'd strike before the colony rose up against him. He was a wasp, goddammit! He could destroy the whole hive if he wanted. Or he could take control of it by destroying the queen. Then, finally: the power he deserved.

He hopped an angry little dance around his living room, buzzing his anger out through his feet and wings. He had to prepare. He had to be sharp, metaphorically; that's what this was all about. The stinger of his mind had to be sharp, ready to fight the queen and assume his rightful place!

He danced faster and faster, circling his couch, every part of him vibrating now. He must be sharp, sharp enough to bore into the queen, to penetrate her. He had to take his rightful place, take the queen. His whole body buzzed with desire.

He stopped dancing abruptly and shook his head. No, it was all supposed to be about his mind. *Sharpen your mind,* he told himself, trying to still his quivering body. But his heart kept pounding, and his stinger ached.

And wasn't mental preparation only half of a warrior's readiness? Wasn't physical preparation also necessary?

I must be sharp.

He sat down on the couch, stinger in hand.

I must be sharp.

He closed his eyes.

It must be sharp.

He leaned back and sharpened his stinger, each stroke bringing him closer to victory.

Marie thought she'd held it together pretty well the rest of the day, considering. Bobby had slept most of the afternoon, and the children had played with the neighbor kids. At dinner she'd forced herself to swallow the soup instead of straining the broth out through her baleen. But Bobby had been agitated. He'd rushed through the meal and was now hustling the kids off to bed while she dunked her fins into the dishwater to wash up. That was his way, he wouldn't say what was bothering him until the kids were in bed.

She heard Bobby step into the kitchen behind her. "Honey," he said to her back, "we need to talk."

He knows, she thought. *He knows I've gone crazy, and he's worried about the kids.* She wrapped the dishtowel around her flippers to keep them from shaking.

He turned her gently by the shoulders to face him. "Honey—"

"Bobby, I know I've been a little out of it today, but—"

"Marie, I'm scared." Creases were scored into the sugar under his eyes.

She gulped. "You're scared of me?"

"What? No, why would I—honey, I think there's something wrong with me."

She put down the towel and led him into the living room, teetering on her tail. "Tell me," she said, pulling him down next to her on the couch.

"Marie, honey, ever since the picnic today, I've been—I haven't been right." He scratched the back of his neck with a paw and looked at her miserably. "I'm seeing things."

"What kind of things?" she croaked.

"Well, it's—I see people differently. Like, not as *people*."

"Like how?" she said, hoping her eagerness sounded like empathy.

"Well, little Bobby Jr. looks like a—like a sausage."

"A sausage?"

"Yeah, like a plump little sausage."

Marie tried not to show the relief trickling through her. Crazy is better shared.

"Not one of those wrinkly brown Jimmy Dean things," he went on, "or those nasty, bloated sausages in a glass jar. No, he's a healthy, pink, little sausage-man."

She nodded. She could see where he got that image.

"And Lisa," he said, "I kinda see her like Tinkerbell. You know, tiny and sweet, sugar and spice, but with a feisty side to her too."

Marie smiled. "She does have her moments."

Bobby shook his head firmly. "No, you don't understand; this isn't just how I imagine their personalities. It's how I actually see them. Literally." Sugar sifted onto his lap as he wrung his hands.

"Honey, it's not just you." She put a flipper on his shoulder. "I've been seeing strange things too, since the picnic." She told him about seeing her Honeypot and Sweetpea and the cloud of children flying around the park and Mr. Evans slithering over the ground and Ms. Hart flying off on her broom. The more lunacy she revealed to him, the more relieved he looked.

He hugged her tight. "We're not crazy! It's not us; there's something at that park."

"What, you mean like some kind of fumes? Toxic waste?" She looked into his shining, ursine face, and he put a paw to her cheek. It felt too real to be an illusion.

"I don't know, Marie. Fumes should have worn off by now, and toxic waste—it wouldn't be this fast. If only we knew—" His eyes flashed with an idea. "Lisa saw a sign at the park, by the lake," he said.

"What lake? I never saw a lake."

"I didn't either, but that pack of Tasmanian devils ripped all through the park." His mouth slanted into a tiny smile. "What you saw as butterflies, I saw as those Loony Tunes Tasmanian devils. Anyway, Lisa saw this sign and wanted me to come read it to her."

"What did it say?"

"I don't know," he sighed. "I didn't look, I just wanted to get out of there. But I'll bet there was something at the lake."

They searched the internet for over an hour, looking for environmental reports, maps of outbreaks, any indication of suspicious activity at the park. Nothing came up.

"We have to go out there," said Bobby.

"Honey, it's the middle of the night. The kids are asleep, and the park's probably closed anyway."

"We'll stay in the car," he said. "I just want to drive around it. The kids can sleep in the back."

"Look, maybe we should just go to the doctor to-morrow—"

"And then what? Get—diagnosed? Let them lock us up in the loony bin and take our kids away?"

Marie's stomach clenched. Nothing had made sense all day, but she was clear on this: no one was going to take her children from her.

Lavinia Hart snarled and prowled around her pent-house. She'd been visualizing her next change for an hour. By now she should have turned into something ferocious and immense, but nothing was happening.

She growled in disgust. She was penned in; she had to get out, run, think. But first, just in case, she rummaged around her closet for her old opera cloak. She rose to her hind legs and threw it around her shoulders, then summoned the elevator. As she rode down to the lobby, she thought about the lecherous night guard Danny, who would most likely be at the security desk. Such a slimy little wretch, always ogling her when she walked by, especially if she happened to bring someone home. Sometimes, if her guest were female, she would toy with him, slipping an arm around the woman's waist or whis-pering into her ear as they sauntered past his desk. She knew Danny would spend the rest of his shift in agony, wishing he were in the middle of his living wet dream in her penthouse.

The elevator doors opened, and Lavinia raised her hood. She really should focus on her transformation, but—she couldn't resist a little fun.

"Good evening, Danny," she purred. She faced away from the desk as she passed, pretending to admire the art on the opposite wall.

"Ms. Hart," he said.

"Interesting," she said, stopping in front of the painting. "You know me without even seeing my face."

"Oh, I'd recognize that voice anywhere."

She almost laughed at his smarmy tone.

"It's awfully late for a lady to be heading out alone," he said. "Lots of crazy people out there."

"Really?" she asked, her voice throaty and low.

"Dangerous people," he said, lowering his voice as well.

She stood in front of the painting, her back to him, and listened to his breathing.

"I'll be quite safe, Danny," she purred, pulling her cloak tighter to accentuate her slender waist. He wouldn't see her tail and legs unless he stood up behind the desk, and she knew he was too lazy for that. "Dangerous people don't frighten me."

"Is that so?" he said, his voice husky.

"Oh, yes," she breathed. "Dangerous people can be very interesting, don't you think? I mean, don't you find it—" She licked her muzzle. "—irresistible when someone takes a risk? Does something they've never done before?"

Lavinia tugged her hood farther down over her face, then angled slightly toward Danny. "Haven't *you* ever wanted to take a risk?" she asked, working a tiny moan into her voice. "Do something you've never done before?"

Danny took in a deep, trembling breath.

She purred and kept her head down, feigning coyness as she stepped closer to the security desk. His chair creaked. Her purr deepened into a growl.

"Ms. Hart?" His breathing was heavy now, his tone uncertain.

Her growl rumbled and grew. Slowly, deliberately, Lavinia placed a paw on top of the desk and clawed. Wood shavings curled up under her nails and fell to the floor.

"What the—"

She lunged at Danny, throwing back her hood with a massive roar. He yelled and jumped up from his chair; a metal wastepaper basket clanged to the floor. Lavinia's roar turned into laughter when he fell back hard into his chair. The chair tipped over, and he fell with it, hitting his head against a credenza before crumpling to the floor.

Lavinia's laugh stuck in her throat.

Danny didn't stir.

"Danny!" she said sharply, leaning over him.

But he didn't move. He lay perfectly still as blood seeped from his head and pooled on the floor.

Marie and Bobby bundled up their children and put them in the back seat. Bobby Jr. whimpered as they backed out of the driveway, but he fell asleep again as soon as they hit the road.

"Lisa hardly even woke up," whispered Marie, after they'd driven a few minutes.

"She spun herself out at the picnic."

Marie smiled. He still hadn't told her what he saw when he looked at her. Maybe he didn't want to say. "So, how do you see yourself?" she asked instead.

"Oh," he said, turning the wheel, "kinda like Paul Bunyan—with a bit of a beer gut. You know, after retirement." He patted his belly with a grunt.

She could imagine it, actually. A paunchy Paul Bunyan, former American folk hero. Big and tall, his muscles a little on the flabby side, but still strong. He'd be carrying an axe jauntily over his shoulder; perhaps a lock of salt and pepper hair would peek out from under his red knit cap.

But, god, did that make her ol' Babe the gimpy Blue Ox?

"So?" he asked. "How do you see yourself?"

She looked down at her folds of blubber stuffed into the front seat of their Caravan. "Oh, you know…" She squinted at the map on his iPhone and asked, "You sure we're going the right way?"

"Yeah, we're almost…" He slowed down and picked up the phone. "Huh. It says we're here."

"What?" She looked around her, but there was no sign of a park anywhere.

He pulled over and poked at the phone. "Yeah, I plugged in the same thing as this morning, and it says we're here."

"But this isn't the park," she said. All she saw was a normal residential neighborhood. The houses were small but neat, with reasonably well-tended lawns and a basketball hoop here and there.

"Look, there it is," whispered Bobby. He pulled out and drove around the corner. Ahead of them stood a ten-foot wall of cypress trees. The entrance was merely the absence of one tree, through which they could see a field of grass about the size of a football field.

Bobby pulled up right in front of the gap and parked. "There's a little pond in the middle of it, see?"

Moonlight glinted off the water.

"Stay here with the kids," he whispered, unlatching his seatbelt.

"Bobby!" she hissed, but he was out of the car before she could object. She glanced back at their sleeping children and watched him through the gap in the trees. He crossed over the grass toward the water. Once at the pond he circled it halfway, staring into the rippling surface. He went down on all fours, and the moonlight from the pond reflected up onto his profile.

"Bobby," she whispered. Something didn't seem right. The light coming up from the water was awfully bright.

He leaned over the sparkling pond and reached toward it with his paw. The tips of his claws ruffled the water's smooth surface, then his whole paw went in up to the wrist.

"Bobby?" She stepped out of the car. Was the pond shrinking?

Bobby's front leg disappeared into the pond up to the elbow. He struggled against something underneath the surface. Suddenly, with a jerk, his whole body slipped under the water.

Legs twitching, Ansel grunted and pulled at his stinger. His flight muscles pulsed at his back. He leaned forward, and his wings, which had been trapped between his body and the couch, popped free and buzzed frantically. He crouched over his stinger, arm pumping. It had to be sharp, sharp, sharp. It had to be perfect and sharpsharpsha—

Crack!

He froze. He stared at his hand in the air, holding his stinger—which was no longer attached to his body.

Crack!

A spasm rocked his body, and a line split down the middle of his chest.

Crack!

Fissures seared across Ansel's body like lines of fire. He panted and clawed at his chest as it bulged. His wings detached and twitched on the couch beside him, crushing themselves into brittle plates. Tufts of white hair popped through chinks of exoskeleton sloughing from his body. His middle legs dropped off, and the remaining four split open to reveal furry mammalian legs.

Ansel's buzzy screams turned into a high, whining squeal. He slid off the couch and rolled into a fetal position on the ground, squealing through the burning and cracking. Finally the pain subsided, leaving him curled and panting on the floor.

As he gained strength, he blinked his eyes open and coughed. He groaned—which sounded like a whimpering squeak—and pulled himself up to a sitting position. Holding his breath, he looked down and explored his new body with small, pink, claw-like hands.

White fur. Twitchy nose with whiskers. Long, naked tail.

"Oh god," he said in a quavering falsetto. He put his paws over his eyes and groaned again. Here he was cracking up, and all he could think to do was sit there and "sharpen his stinger." And look where that had gotten him.

Ansel surveyed the bits of antennae and exoskeleton scattered around him, catching a glimpse of something glinting under a piece of wing. He rolled over on all fours and sifted through the debris to uncover it. It was a silver sword! He lifted it to feel its heft, then stood up on his hind legs and held it to the light. It was a beauty, with scrolling inscriptions etched into the base and a leather hilt studded with emeralds and rubies.

He touched a finger to its edge and pulled his paw back with a sharp intake of breath. This one didn't need sharpening.

He lay the sword on his couch and stared at it. What could all of this mean? The symbolism of the wasp and the queen bee was clear; he could see what his brain was doing there. But what the hell was a mouse with a sword supposed to mean?

There was only one place to find out, back to where it had all started.

Back to Mirror Pond Park.

"Danny, get up," hissed Lavinia, shaking him. "Wake up."

Finally he groaned. She cursed with relief as he moaned and held his head. Paws trembling, she knocked the handset off the phone and tapped out 911 with her claw. As soon as the person answered, she threw the receiver down to Danny and ran outside.

What the hell was she doing? She'd almost killed a man, almost gotten herself embroiled in a murder, and for what? Because he was a little creepy, and she felt like a laugh? Well, he was moving and talking—moaning at least. Hopefully he wouldn't remember what had happened.

And if he did, no one would believe him anyway.

She had to stay focused, but she couldn't. She was panicking, running a loop around the same block until the sound of sirens knocked her out of her absurdly close orbit.

What was she doing? Of course they'd find her. They'd have security footage, the clawmarks on the desk, perhaps pawprints on the phone. He'd looked her full in the face before he fell. There had been confusion and disbelief in his eyes. Terror. And lust.

Lavinia kept running, paws pounding, cape flowing along her back. She sought out deserted alleys, then abandoned them to slip across darkened lawns. Finally she caught on to where her body was leading her. Of course. It was exactly where she needed to be.

With a fresh burst of speed, she headed toward Mirror Pond Park.

Marie called out to Bobby, but he didn't resurface. She tumbled out of the Caravan and toddled toward him on her ridiculously tiny flukes. The pond was growing smaller and smaller—she'd never make it to him in time. Marie jumped in desperation, and suddenly she was swimming in the air, undulating through the park. She zeroed in on the shrinking pond, and with a flip of her tail, slipped past the grassy banks into the water.

The bright light she'd seen before was gone. Only a sliver of moonlight penetrated the water, but she didn't need even that. Heart pounding, she wheeled and tasted the water, alert for traces of sugar. Instead, she sensed heat and felt bubbles. Marie dove toward the source and found Bobby back in human form, unconscious and sinking. She swam underneath him and nosed him up to the surface, horrified by how quickly the grassy edges were moving inward. With a flip of her head, she tossed her husband out of the lake, then tried to wriggle herself out onto the muddy bank.

But she was too heavy. She couldn't even flop halfway up, and the banks were closing in. The more she churned against the silt, the faster it moved. She could dive down and gather enough momentum to jump out of the water—but would the hole be too small by then?

"Marie, jump!"

It was Bobby. He was on his hands and knees, fighting the water, clawing away great clumps of mud and grass.

She submerged once again and wheeled around. With a thrust of her tail, she shot up toward the surface. Silt clouded the water, but she could see the moonlight above, and she could hear Bobby calling to her. She thrashed her tail and tensed her body for one final swish. She jumped. Her nose broke the surface and her body rose out of the pond, arcing to the side. Mud and grass streaked her flanks as she cleared the water and thundered down onto the grass. A shower erupted from her blowhole, soaking Bobby.

"Hang on," he said, and lifted her tail out of the water. The grass closed in on itself, and the last of the pond disappeared, leaving only a grimy puddle of mud.

He dropped down next to her as she lay panting on the grass, and they held each other until they both stopped trembling.

Marie turned her head toward the Caravan. She could still see it through the gap in the trees, but it was too dark to see inside. Bobby jumped up, jogged to the van, and peered through the windows. "Still asleep," he reported, walking back to where she lay.

He knelt beside her and helped her sit up. "Look at this," he said, and pressed a seashell into her flipper. Moonlight reflected off a mirror embedded in it. She turned the shell over and examined the back. It was ivory-colored, about 6 inches wide, scalloped with deep ridges. She ran the tip of her flipper over a little rectangular patch that had been smoothed into the surface. Words were etched into it, but it was too dark to read them.

Bobby flipped the shell so the mirror faced her again. "Look how beautiful you are in the moonlight."

She held the mirror away and cast her eyes down.

"Look," he insisted, guiding her flipper back.

She raised her eyes and saw—her own face. Her own, honest-to-god human face, with wet ringlets of hair hanging down around her astonished eyes.

"But—" she sputtered. She angled the mirror down her body, incredulous. With her own eyes she saw a blubbery grey whale, but looking into the mirror, she saw neither a whale nor the dull, frumpy mother-of-two she'd been before. According to the shell, she was a mermaid, and a damn sexy one at that.

Marie flicked her tail and stared at the fleshy, curvy body in the glass, wondering at its shimmering scales and the ample breasts almost popping out of the pale pink shells covering them.

"Is this really how you see me?" she breathed, not daring to look away from the mirror.

Bobby turned her face gently toward his. She held her breath as his lips met hers. She tried to sink into the kiss, but felt a fresh surge of despair when she sensed his tongue playing at the baleen in her mouth. God, how could he want this?

She tried to pull away, but Bobby held her. His tongue pushed through the strands of baleen and sought out hers, and he ran his hands down her fat, clammy body as though she were the most beautiful thing in the world. That's how he saw her, after all, and she willed herself to believe it too. But her fins felt wet and slimy on his shirt, and she was revolted by her own huge tongue rolling around after his.

"Stop," she said, pushing him away. "We need to get the kids home." She stood up, not wanting to see the hurt on his face. At least she felt steadier on her tail now. Maybe she would get used to this.

She lumbered through the trees and stopped short. There, inside the van, Lisa and Bobby Jr. were asleep— in human form.

Bobby gripped her flipper. "They're back, Marie!" He hugged her tight.

He smiled and held her flipper all the way home. She should be happy: Bobby was Bobby again, the kids were back, everything was coming into place again—except her. She sat quietly, trying to feel hopeful as Bobby steered away from the park, through the streets and up their driveway.

We're all back home, she thought. Everyone but me.

She held little Bobby Jr., not a Honeypot, and watched the real Bobby carry the real Lisa up the driveway. Tears fogged her vision as she tottered behind them on her flukes. How long would she be like this?

They put the kids back in their beds, and Marie cleaned out her blowhole with a Q-tip while Bobby brushed his teeth. As she climbed into bed, she noticed he'd put the shell mirror on her bedside table. She picked it up and looked into it as she slid under the covers, preferring the reflection of the mermaid to her own grey bulk.

She turned the shell over and read the inscription:

SPECULUM CREDE

Bobby came to bed and put an arm around her waist. She showed him the words.

"What does this mean?"

"I don't know," he said, reaching over her to turn out the light. "We'll look it up tomorrow."

She held the shell in her flipper and let him snuggle up to her. She usually didn't like him spooning her; hated the thought of his beefy palm being dwarfed by her post-childbirth stomach. She normally spooned him instead, her fleshy arms around him, her soft belly filling in the space between them.

But tonight she let him put his arms around her and whisper into her ear, "Everything will be fine tomorrow."

She wanted to believe him.

The key to Lavinia's next transformation lay in Mirror Pond Park; she knew it. She ran toward it with a sense of purpose, stopping only to duck behind a bush as some yuppie drove by in a Prius. She sped between two trees into a field and wheeled around, baffled. This was the place. She knew she was in the right place, but nothing looked the same. It was just a field surrounded by cypress trees; no picnic benches, no playset, nothing like what she'd seen that morning.

She loped out to the middle of the field. The grass was wet, and getting wetter with every step. Her left front paw sank into a pocket of mud. She wriggled it until it came up with a slurpy, sucking sound, but then her right front paw got stuck. By the time she pulled it free, both her rear paws were lodged in slimy, cold silt. She shifted her weight, only to find both front paws stuck again as well.

Lavinia had barely noticed the pounding of her heart while running, but now each thump shook her chest. The more she pulled, the lower she sank. Her breathing turned rapid and shallow, and she began to feel light-headed. She told herself not to panic, but couldn't stop writhing and bucking deeper into the mud.

Somewhere behind her, she heard a *squeak,* something that sounded almost like pleasure. She froze, sucking her stomach in over the silt.

"Lavinia, is that you?"

She twisted her head. A white mouse holding a silver sword strolled into view.

"Lavinia. It's Ansel."

Relief flooded through her. "Ansel, thank god you're here. Help me out of this." Who cared that he was a mouse and that he'd called her by her first name? They'd deal with all that after he pulled her free.

But he didn't move. He just stood and looked at her.

"Ansel!" she called again. What the hell was he doing? She tried to free a paw to reach him, then gasped in fresh shock as her warm belly touched clammy mud.

The mouse let out an ugly, screeching laugh. "Ah, Lavinia, I finally see you as you really are: frightened, stuck, and alone."

The words hit her like a slap. "Ansel, help me."

"Help you?" he pondered, stroking his chin with his paw.

She growled and bucked again until the cold slime was halfway up her flanks. "Hurry!"

"Help you," he said again. "The way you've helped me all these years?"

"Ansel, please."

His voice was shrill. "Stuck all these years, doing your bidding as a 'Director' while others rose to 'Vice President' around me?"

She growled and seethed in the mud. "Are you really going to let me die like this because of a workplace grudge?"

Ansel cocked his head. "No, I shouldn't do that, should I? Just passively let you sink. No, that wouldn't be very brave of me at all." He raised the tip of his sword and pointed it at her heart. "Here, let me free you." He glared into her eyes and took a step forward.

A wave of anger flared from her gut and filled her entire body. She roared, and her hips and tail slipped below the surface. She barely noticed the chill.

Ansel's eyes widened for a moment. Then he stilled the quivering point of his sword and took another step toward her. He looked down and peeled his paw up from the mud.

"I see," he said, stepping backward. "It seems I'll just need to let you finish the job yourself."

Heat seared through Lavinia. A bubble erupted next to her in the mud, spewing a whiff of sulfur. Another bubble rose and popped. She heard sizzling and smelled something burning, like hair. And flesh. Mud bubbled around her, and small tufts of grass burst into flame. Through the steam, she saw Ansel drop the tip of his sword to the ground and stagger back.

She felt herself growing, her arms and legs expanding, her field of vision lifting above the pit of grass and mud. Muscles strained and pulled at her back, and her beautiful fur fell away from her body in flaming strips. She roared in pain, and was in ecstasy at the horrific new sound she made. It was like lions and eagles and engines and thunder all at once. It was the sound of a beautiful death—but not hers.

Lavinia flexed her muscles and pulled her massive, leathery wings up out of the mud. She stretched them wide and admired their strong, black spines and the curved, cruel-looking talons at their ends. After a few exploratory wingbeats, she trained her eyes on the small, white mouse trembling at the edge of the field. Bracing herself on the ends of her wings, she pulled the rest of her long, platy body up from the bog.

The mouse raised his sword, trembling but resolute. His eyes locked on one part of her body, as though he were afraid to take in the whole of her. Yet he dared to approach, and Lavinia curved in a semicircle around him as his shivering legs brought him closer.

The little white warrior advanced, pivoting to track the same spot on her body as she flanked him. He was obviously too terrified to look her in the eyes. And yet he did not run. Lavinia wound steadily around him, mesmerizing him, until she had completely encircled him with her armored girth.

My little Ansel must have a deathwish.

She would have felt sorry for him, if he hadn't been content to let her suffocate in the mud. Worse yet, he would have killed her himself if he'd been able to reach her. She circled him again, doubling the coils around him. She could strike at any time, but she wanted to prolong this; enjoy it. She was a massive beast with claws, teeth, probably even fire, although she hadn't tried it yet. What could he possibly do to her?

With a pitiful screech, Ansel tightened his grip on his sword and barreled toward her. She looked down to see where he was heading, and roared in shock. Even if she could breathe fire, he was so close she would hit herself too. She shifted in preparation for flight, but he moved with her and kept running toward the mouse-sized chink in her armor.

Lavinia had no choice. She drew in a great gust of air and prepared for her first breath of flame.

Marie gasped awake. Her heart was pounding, and she was twisted up in a knot of damp sheets. But no, she was not burned to a crisp.

And she was no longer a whale.

She held her breath, and her fingers—fingers!—explored her sweaty face and damp hair.

"Honey!" she whispered.

Bobby snored. She'd pulled all the sheets off him, but he was still sound asleep.

"Honey, I'm—" She ran her hands down both arms, up both legs. Was she really back?

She felt around for the shell mirror, but couldn't find it. She untangled her legs from the sheets and ran to the bathroom, stubbing her toe—her toe!—on the clothes hamper. She flicked on the light and squinted in the sudden brightness at her own familiar, ordinary, wonderful face. She touched her cheeks, her nose, her ears, everything, to make sure it was real.

A gleam caught her eye. With careful fingers, she picked a shining scale out of her hair. She put it in her palm and tipped her hand side to side, watching the scale catch the light.

Marie clicked off the light and tiptoed down the hall to check on Lisa and Bobby Jr. She lingered in the doorway for a while, rubbing her finger against the scale in her palm and listening to her children sigh in their sleep.

Calmer now, she stepped back down the hall toward her bedroom. She hesitated by the bathroom, then went inside. She turned on the tap and washed the gleaming scale down the drain.

Back in her bedroom, she saw that Bobby had kicked the sweaty sheets off their bed. She grabbed a fresh blanket and lay down next to him, spooning him as she covered them both. He rumbled in his sleep and grasped the arm she put around his waist. She breathed in deeply, her nose at his back. He smelled warm and sweet.

"I had a nightmare," she whispered.

"Mm-mmm," he mumbled, barely awake.

"It was about a little white mouse with a sword fighting a huge, firebreathing dragon."

She kissed his back, and he rumbled again.

"But I don't know who won," she said softly. She thought about it for a moment. "I don't think either of them will."

Tomorrow she would update her resume. There was a whole wide world outside Haverton Industries.

Marie kissed Bobby's back again, tasting his skin with the tip of her tongue. He sighed himself awake and rolled toward her. He reached for her, and his tongue was sugar in her mouth.

The Rapture

The Rapture comes at you slant, gets you when you aren't looking. But I know it's coming. The whole town is emptying out, one family at a time.

"Why, John, they're not being raptured." That's what my wife tells me. "You just watched the Johnsons move last weekend. The Rapture doesn't come in a U-Haul truck."

I know how I sound. But how else do you explain all the white people leaving town? It's the Rapture, and it's taking the white people first because all those posters with a blue-eyed, straight-haired Jesus were actually true.

Leena went a little pale herself the first time I told her that part. I knew she wasn't ready to hear it. But we can't keep ignoring it. The Johnsons were the last white family in town. What we don't know is whether the rest of us are next.

The Rapture comes at you oblique, like it isn't paying attention until it is. That said, it's not like it catches you off guard—nobody's disappeared from inside their homes or left empty chairs swiveling at work. No cars have careened off the highway, suddenly devoid of their drivers. Like Leena says, they've all moved away.

They tell us it's for a new job or sick mother, but when we hear them talking amongst themselves:

Safer neighborhood.

Better schools.

Less crime.

They act like it's their own idea, but actually, it's the Rapture.

It's like that fungus, the one that infects insects and takes over their brains. I saw it on a nature show: this fungus needs to be up high to spread its spores, so it gets an ant, say, to think it wants to be up high too, and makes it crawl from the forest floor, where it's relatively safe, to the highest tip of the highest leaf of the biggest plant it can reach. Now, no bug in its right mind should want to be up there, sitting out in the open for any bird flying by to come and snatch, but that's where the fungus makes the ant think it wants to be.

Then, when the ant is as high as it can go, the fungus kills it and keeps growing like a tower, bursting out its head or its back, right through its exoskeleton. That spindle of fungus reaches up and up, and when it's as tall as it can get, it pops, sending its spores out everywhere. And each little spore lands and infects another insect and makes it do this suicidal thing, against all its instincts, climbing up to dangerous heights and then… well, then the whole thing happens all over again.

So, all these people who move away from here, telling themselves it's for something better—is it really? Who actually knows what happens to them when they leave.

"I see them on Facebook," says Leena, and she thinks that settles it. But I'm not so sure. That fungus takes time to grow; they just speed up the footage for the nature shows. That's how it is with the Rapture too.

They'll go where we can't follow, and we'll watch them climb. In real time, the long, slow time you don't see on TV, we'll see updates about promotions, prep schools and clean streets, photos of BMWs and Caribbean vacations, kids graduating Harvard, tow-headed grandchildren. Maybe a boat for the weekends.

But eventually they'll stop and look back, and then, one chink at a time—because remember, it won't be sudden—they'll crack wide open, and then they'll finally find out that the Rapture is nothing like what they thought it would be.

It's not hard to imagine. It probably starts like a headache, a little bit of pressure behind your eyes. Then it spreads, thickening, tendriling itself into your muscles, your organs, your bones, muffling you from the inside. You keep telling yourself you're fine, even though you can't move, think, breathe. Eventually your skin swells and fissures. Splits.

Now, when Leena starts to look desperate at hearing this, I'll admit it: I know it's not really the Rapture. And I know we're not next. But looking up at them, looking down at me, I can feel what it would be like, that pressure building inside, pushing, squeezing, suffocating, until there's nothing left to do but burst wide open.

I know what it is to explode in slow motion.

Lost Kingdom

All around you is inky blackness, yet somehow the feathers of the peacock running ahead of you gleam, iridescent. You're stumbling after it, but you no longer remember where or why. You stop, and the peacock runs off into the gloom.

A moment later, an unearthly squawk drills through the air, followed by a high-pitched series of screeches: *eerh, eerh, eerh, eerh, eerh, eerh.* The birdcall pierces and echoes. It's a jungle sound, exotic and chilling. Then it stops.

Somewhere out in the darkness before you, a shadowy bulk shifts. The outline of some burly animal lumbers toward you, from the same direction the peacock had gone. Somehow you know not to move. Or, that there's nowhere else to go anyway.

A minotaur emerges from the pitch. He's holding the peacock, and as they approach, they are suffused with a brightness as though they were under spotlights. As though they were lights themselves.

"Such a proud bird," says the minotaur, admiring it, stroking its silky throat with a meaty hand. "It always thinks it knows best." His voice is low and rumbling. Soothing.

He looks up from the peacock nestled in the crook of his arm. "Do you think it knows best?" He is quite close now. You feel like a mouse that just discovered the cat hunting in tall grass.

"Well, do you?" he asks again. His breath is rank, like ozone and rot, like swamp baking in sun. You notice then that you're sweating, and breathing too fast, and the minotaur looks spinny, but no, that's just your vision going haywire. Dizziness jellies your knees.

With one arm, the minotaur holds you up. "For the love of your kingdom," he prods. He shakes you once, gently. "Just say it."

I have a kingdom? you want to ask, but his bass murmur lulls you. The gesture reminds you of your father, and you put a hand on his chest to feel the vibration like you did when you were young.

The minotaur steps back and makes you stand on your own. "Answer me," he says. "Is this bird—" and he briefly lifts the peacock, which is watching you— "always right?"

You blink at the bird and back up at the minotaur, and you could swear he looks sad. Your head starts to spin again, and you collapse onto dusty cobblestones. The dirt smells like somewhere you've been on vacation, somewhere foreign and unreal. You catch a whiff of stale beer and gag.

"It's too late, it seems," he says, and lowers the peacock to the ground. "It's won again."

The peacock rushes away, cackling. The clack of its talons on stone reminds you of something. Hooves on a road. Dozens of them.

"What was that all about?" you ask.

The minotaur sighs, and your gaze follows the leisurely swing of his horns as he shakes his head. "That was about you losing your kingdom."

You stare at him. You don't know where you are, or how to get back to where you were, or if this minotaur will decide you're too dumb to let live and turn on you; but somehow the loss of a kingdom you've never seen is all you can think of.

"Don't worry," the minotaur says, as though reading your mind. "You never thought of it as a kingdom anyway."

"But—"

He holds a hand out to stop you. It reminds you of the start of a race you have to win. Had to win. But lost.

"You've battled imaginary enemies all your life," he tells you. "Why quibble now?"

"So, this is just my imagination?" And you know it has to be, because you're hearing things you can't see: a herd of cattle or something snorting behind you.

He tips his head to the side, thinking, and you feel like you've seen this all before, only much, much faster.

"Can I wake up now?" you ask.

The minotaur's horns loop again in a peaceful *no*. A tsunami of pride crashes through you, hubris whooshing down your body just before the blood drains from your face. And now you taste the bile on your tongue, the tang of fear after too many *cervesas* and big talk, you and your fellow gringos strutting down the streets of Pamplona toward a battle no one asked you to fight.

The minotaur's eyes narrow. "I think you see it now, no?"

And it happens just like they say, all those memories flash by like a movie. That one frame where you still had a chance to say no.

"Yes, you see it," the minotaur says. He nods, his horns rising and falling. Rising and falling. "Yes, now you see the kingdom you lost. And for what?"

The Legend of Fog

Long ago, before cell phones and cars, before villages and farming, before hunting and gathering, there was Fog. And she was happy.

She spent her days wandering through mountains and valleys, skimming rivers and lakes, swirling around the planet as she pleased. She loved rolling through forests, savoring the stroke of leaves and the scratch of branches and bark. She lingered over the ocean for hours while its white-capped waves tickled her belly. But her favorite thing was to move among all the animals of the earth. There were big ones with feathers and leathery skin, and small ones with fur that scurried around their feet. Some stretched their necks to graze in trees, others swung their spiky tails and bashed each other. They laid eggs and fed what came out of them, or they spilled tiny copies of themselves directly out of their bodies. These creatures fascinated Fog, and she was sad when the fireballs came and everything changed.

The little hairy creatures survived, but Fog missed the big ones. She missed the feel of their skins and horns as they moved through her, especially the ones who spread their large, spiny wings, high in the sky, and sliced right through her. She was lonely for a long while, having to content herself with watching new mountains push up from the earth, idly scratching herself on a banyan or thorn tree, with only the occasional excitement of earth-quakes and volcanic eruptions.

The small furry creatures multiplied and changed, morphing bit by bit into ever more interesting things. Limbs became flippers or disappeared entirely, tails grew or shrank or vanished, animals decided to walk on two legs, or stay on four, or hang from trees, or slip into and out of the oceans. Watching these transformations, she began to feel quietly happy once more, until one day, everything changed again.

Anubis arrived. And Shiva. And Zeus. And Odin and Ishtar and Quetzalcoatl and Tanno and so many more. Creatures like her, not bound to earth or water. One by one they appeared, filling up the air through which she moved with their singing and dancing, fighting and loving, bearing children and killing them.

Fog was at first alarmed, but she soon became intrigued with these new beings. She moved among them, sweeping against their backs and bellies, winding herself around their legs and claws. She began to test them, compressing herself into different solidities to match their manifestations, observing their reactions when they first perceived her as something more than an odd prickling against their skins. Many of them—Aphrodite, Bes, Astarte, Kama, and Rati—tangled themselves up into her and made love to her. Eventually she gave birth to two daughters, Frost and Dew.

Over time, Fog's new companions became gods. By the time it happened to Bacchus, she had learned to recognize the signs: he looked down toward the earth more often, began to preoccupy himself with the soil-bound animals she would come to know as mankind. Even as he embraced her and tasted her mist, he occasionally stopped and tipped his head as though hearing a far-off call. She knew when he'd visited the humans, could smell their musk on him, taste their wine on his skin, and she knew she would have to share him. One by one, Fog would come to share all of the gods with the humans who claimed them.

Fog watched the various ways in which gods loved their humans. Some of them strafed the earth with their wrath, growing fat and arrogant on the meat of sacrifice. Others coddled their favorites with offspring and riches. A few were distant and aloof, leaving their humans to their own graces and follies. Many made love to their humans, whether they wanted it or not.

The more attention mankind demanded, the more peevish Fog grew. Her companions became too preoccupied with the earth-bound beings to pay proper attention to her. She began to plague the humans, cloaking their eyes and stoking their fears. She hid prey from their arrows and bullets, hid land from their boats when they sailed. She bundled up the howling of wolves and the grunting of bears and the roaring of lions, carried the sounds in her thickness, and encircled cowering villagers with muffled, unknowable menace.

But her interference angered the gods. They wanted no one else to have sway over their humans. They could not banish Fog, but they withdrew from her, refusing her embraces and casting her away from their hearts. With no friends left in the air, she retreated to the earth with Frost and Dew.

Fog consoled herself by showing her daughters the many things to taste and smell and feel on the surface.

Her sadness melted into delight as she discovered her daughters' different natures.

Dew fell in love with grass and trees, pressing herself against them blade by blade, leaf by leaf, throughout the night. Her dislike of humans was even stronger than her mother's, and she fled when they woke at the first light of day.

Frost was bolder, solidifying and clinging to everything in sight. She didn't fear humans; she even taunted them, hanging from their eyelashes and beards if it was cold enough. And if they ignored her too long, she would wriggle through their fabric coverings to nibble on delicate fingers, noses and toes. She wrapped herself around everything, only relenting when the sun made it too hot for her liking.

Winter became their favorite season. Frost and Dew made a friend named Wind. No one knew where he came from. They laughed as they ran together through the trees, rattling empty nests and kicking dead leaves before them. Fog watched them gleefully swirl and paint windows and rooftops and fences and bushes and whole fields of dried cornstalks. The faster Wind ran, the colder it stayed, and the fewer people ventured outside. Fog was delighted.

Until.

Until Fog noticed her daughter Frost lingering at a certain windowpane. Wind and Dew teased her, but she persisted, building up nightly at one particular window of the castle of the King of Twain.

Fog knew better than to ask, waiting instead until Frost left the window on a warm afternoon. Fog peeked through the glass and saw a young man sitting at a desk.

He wore an elaborate crimson tunic edged in gold. A prince, likely. He was writing a letter, and when he looked up from the page, Fog felt a pang of loss—the youth's large eyes and full lips reminded her of Bacchus. The young man pushed back from his table and crossed his muscular legs. She could well understand her daughter's fascination with this man, but hoped it would not move beyond observation.

She decided to watch this prince more carefully—for her daughter's safety, of course, she told herself. When Frost was at the window, which was often, Fog scrutinized the rest of his clan. She saw how the king leered at his sons' brides and wheedled himself into their chambers while their husbands were hunting; how on other nights he would send for a poor young maid in the village, seducing her via messenger with promises of gold for her family and marriage to his youngest, unwed son; how his son remained unwed despite all the hopeful village girls who visited the king's bed. The Queen knew of all this, but instead of asserting herself like Hera, she meekly accepted things as they were. Watching this family, Fog often found herself missing the clarity of the gods, their open love and retribution, the uncloaked multiplicity of their hearts. The world she'd been frozen out of.

When Fog could get a glimpse of the prince, he always seemed to be occupied with correspondence. He read and wrote long letters, running his fingers over them with a slight smile on his face. When he finished writing he would seal his missives with wax and a kiss before calling a messenger to bring them out into the world.

Fog followed the messenger once, trailing his horse as it galloped through fields, across rivers, and over hills. The letter traveled through several messengers' hands until it reached the lap of a young seamstress who lived in a cottage with her father and sisters. The father smiled proudly, the sisters giggled and clapped, and the seamstress put down her sewing and clasped the letter to her breast. Once she finished the letter, she carefully placed it in a box of identical papers and hugged her family.

Fog didn't need to see any more. Indeed, by the time she got back to the castle, Frost was whirling around it in a rage. She crazed the windows with thick sheets of ice, froze the gutters, and caked the doors shut. Dew hovered helplessly by; Wind had long since rushed away.

"Mother," Frost sobbed. "He's going to marry!" She rushed up to Fog as though she'd had something to do with it.

Fog bundled herself around her girl, caressing her and wiping chips of ice away from her cheeks.

"We heard them," said Dew. "The prince and his father. Arguing."

"Arguing?" asked Fog.

"Yes. We heard the king yelling and came to see why. That's when we heard: the prince intends to ask the hand of some village girl in marriage. The king will not allow it, because his son has been promised to the Princess of Wix."

"Daughter, perhaps it is for the best," she said. "From what I've observed of humans, deceit and unhappiness are all that come of marital union."

The idea of marriage had always appalled Fog. Only one partner for the rest of one's days? And how could they know they were compatible if they hadn't yet made love?

"Mother's right," Dew said. "Better that this fate befall some human princess than you."

But Frost was inconsolable. She buried herself in her mother's softness and cried, her tears dropping shards of ice upon the earth.

"Darling, it really is for the best. Yes, this prince has many talents, and he is beautiful. But his father, the king, brings doom upon his house."

"Mother," Frost sniffed. "You're simply angry that the gods have been so generous with these humans instead of paying attention to us."

Fog bristled. "It is true that the gods should take more of an interest in their daughters." She released Frost and thinned herself to quell her anger. "But that has nothing to do with it. This king flouts human rules as though above them and abuses the gifts his god gave him. He elevates himself, thinks of himself as a god—and eventually he and his clan will suffer his god's wrath."

"You're wrong, Mother." Frost's voice sliced through her. "You're just jealous of the gods' love. But I refuse to live in bitterness. I'm going to win the prince's heart and take my rightful place at his side!" She wiped the last ice chips from her cheeks and swirled away.

Dew stretched herself uncertainly between Fog and the departing Frost. "Look after her," said Fog, and with that, Dew trailed off after her sister.

For a moment, Fog thought about following them and telling them everything she'd seen: the king's leering and wheedling, his false promises to village girls, his sons' ignorance of their wives' acquiescence, the queen's spineless acceptance of it all. Such a clan, with its over-weening king, impotent men, and weak-willed women, was no place for a daughter of hers. But she knew Frost was too angry to listen just then.

Fog would soon discover, however, that Frost had not merely stormed off in a fit of anger. Had she known of her daughter's plan, she probably would have inter-vened to save the Princess of Wix, whose boat sank in a storm as it crossed the normally placid lake between the two kingdoms. The storm, it was said, was a sudden, lethal confluence of freezing rain and gale force winds.

When Fog confronted them, Dew scattered to the fields, and Wind whisked away. Frost, however, crack-led proudly.

"That girl did you no harm," Fog told her.

"Such considerations," sneered Frost, "have never troubled the gods, nor you. And so, they shall not trou-ble me."

Fog wrapped herself around her daughter. "Nothing good can come of such rancor."

"You said yourself, nothing good will come to this house anyway." Frost spun out of her mother's embrace and eddied carelessly across the castle grounds. "Why should a little storm make things worse?"

"Have you not seen what the king does with his other sons' brides?"

Frost went still for a moment. "He will not bother me," she decided, and kept spinning.

"And you see honor in his seduction of the poorest young women of his kingdom? You want to be part of that lineage?"

Frost stopped again. "I will freeze him out of their hearts." And once again she danced, twirling up and down the castle walls, leaving a fine coat of ice behind her.

The prince, undeterred, kept writing letters to his fair seamstress in the village. Frost tried to intervene, but Dew and Wind feared Fog's wrath after what they'd done to the princess of Wix, and they refused to help her again.. Without their assistance, all Frost could do was make the trip uncomfortable for the messengers.

Each day the sun shone a little longer and warmer. Fog made no effort to shield her daughter from the heat, and eventually Frost gave up her efforts with the prince, preferring to spend her time in cooler climes north of the kingdom.

As flowers bloomed and fresh grass surged up from the earth, letters flowed freely between the prince and his love in the village. The king finally relented to their engagement. They would be married in the fall.

Frost stayed away from the Kingdom of Twain all summer. She wouldn't even enter the same landmass. Fog could hardly blame her. Her daughter wouldn't have wanted to see the calligraphers penning invitations on thick parchment, messengers delivering the scrolls to castles far and wide, regal garments being sewn, or cows and pigs being fattened for the feast. The bride-to-be, so talented and industrious was she, sewed a velveteen suit for her father. She designed her own bridal gown, and was so modest she had to be talked into making it even more beautiful than the visions she had created for her mother and sisters. Jewelers, enchanted, showered her with diamonds and pearls, each one vying to be the one to bedeck the charming princess-to-be.

No, thought Fog, it would have done her daughter no good at all to have witnessed any of this.

Frost returned just before the wedding, but didn't last long amongst the flourishes of flutes and horns rehearsing. She barely had time to wilt a few flowers in the bride's bouquet before fleeing the flutter of bridesmaids' skirts. The flowers were quickly replaced, the guests' coaches arrived, and that afternoon the humble village girl became a princess.

The celebration reverberated across the kingdom: cheers went up, mugs were raised, even the thriftiest farmer granted himself an extra portion of bread. There were, however, some dozens of huts where peasant girls silently raged over honor and promises broken. No matter how quietly they mourned, Fog heard them all.

Over days and weeks, the headiness subsided and life in the kingdom returned to normal. The days grew shorter and cooler, and Frost returned. She looked into the prince's bedroom window, once, then meticulously coated every rose in the queen's garden.

The king grew restless with the increasingly longer nights. His new daughter-in-law could not be seduced, which emboldened his other son's wives to refuse him as well. And so he turned back to the village. Not having his son's hand to barter, he turned to coercion. His messengers rode out from the castle with sinister bargains: a father in prison or a night with the king; if not you, your little sister.

These weren't the worst horrors Fog had seen on earth. What plagued her was that Frost couldn't stay away from the castle. Every morning the palace minders had to chip away layers of ice from the windows and doors.

"Frost, darling," Fog said at last. "Why do you waste yourself on this wretched family?"

Frost dawdled, coating the flags on the castle's spires until they crackled. Dew and Wind sighed, accidentally snapping the fabric into shards.

"All right, then," said Fog. "Listen, all of you. I've got a plan."

Fog whispered to Frost and Dew and Wind, whirling them up into her vision for the king.

That night a mysterious traveler approached the castle grounds. Her eyes shone like starlight from the shadows of her hood. She breezed past the drawbridge guards in her purple cloak, beguiling them with a coquettish smile. The guards at the entrance to the inner grounds bowed toward her swishing ebony skirts, opening the doors wide at her approach. She swept past footmen and attendants, halting them in attitudes of bewildered admiration.

The traveler knew exactly where to go. She passed through the queen's garden of dead roses and mounted the thick stone steps to the private chambers.

She found the king in his bedroom, lounging on a leather divan and reading a book of Norse myth. His footman had simply opened the door and stepped aside to let her enter. When questioned later, the footman would not be able to describe her concretely. He could only tell of her regal assurance, her utmost grace, and the oddly piercing chill wafting from her silken garb. He wouldn't be able to say why he was not alarmed when she closed the door behind her, shutting him out. He somehow felt—and this he revealed to no one—that something good and just was about to occur. The footman would describe the creak of leather, the click of the king's step across the room, heavy breathing and the rustle of skirts, the croaking joints of the sovereign's bedframe. And then a whoosh. A crackle. A crash. The cacophony of a thousand mirrors breaking.

The footman yanked open the door and rushed into a spinning cauldron of snow. The smoke of freshly extinguished candles stung his eyes; curtains and bedlinens whipped in the acrid wind. All the windows were shattered, and moonlight streamed in through gaping, empty arches, glinting off shards of glass embedded in sparkling snowdrifts.

The king was nowhere to be seen.

A massive search ensued, with baying dogs and knights on horseback. A week passed, then two, then months. At a year, the queen announced the king's death. So refined and graceful was her mourning, it almost seemed like happiness. When her eldest son became king, he donated chests of gold to the village sanctuary housing young women with children born outside of marriage.

From that day forward, the kingdom of Twain was a place of endless spring, bathed in perpetual sunshine. Wind included the realm in his rounds, but Fog and her daughters, Frost and Dew, found their happiness in other lands. They glided and danced under crystalline northern skies. They undulated with auroras of pink and green, yellow and blue. They joined in many a hunt, riffling white fur, whistling through antlers, and winding around glistening fangs. They hung daggers from rooftops and watched them melt in the spring.

Most nights were so dark and clear, Fog could look up and see the contours of her once-familiar gods roiling above. She remembered the ages of sliding between them, over their skins, firming and diffusing, entering and being entered. Odin looked down at her briefly—not long, but long enough. She would unfreeze their hearts again. One day, she knew, she would leave her daughters, hover over a sunbaked vineyard, and call out for Bacchus. He would reach out and breathe her in.

Midnight at the Organporium

I only did it for you, when I crept into the Organporium at the Southside Mall last night and broke the glass to the heart display and took what I thought you needed. I mean, how could I have known it wasn't the right thing? I'd watched you and listened to you; I'd felt your hands on my shoulders pushing me away, what you called *keeping a comfortable distance*. I'd observed you from that uncomfortable distance, and I thought I knew exactly what was missing.

I was thinking of you when I crouched in the darkened Organporium and looked at all those hearts lined up in their clear plastic boxes. My own heart was beating so fast and loud, I was sure all the hearts in the refrigerated display case could hear it. I imagined them, stacked up as many as three high on each shelf, each one throbbing at the same manic speed as mine. I thought maybe I should grab two: one for you, plus a spare for my own abused original.

I figured a siren was already going off, a silent one, because all I heard was the blood in my ears as I crept up to the case (I was wearing my black ballet flats for stealth, along with black everything else) and cracked the display's glass with my elbow. I tried to pad my elbow with my shirt, but it wasn't big enough to cover and swing at the same time, which is odd, because you always say my shirts are too baggy, and I should try wearing a dress sometime. I wound up having to take off my shirt to protect my elbow, which still wasn't enough. I smashed the glass with a chair, then swiped the broken pieces out of the pane with my shirt over my hand; but there were too many shards stuck in the shirt to put it back on, which explains why I'm wearing a white Orioles T-shirt with a black bra showing through in that picture all the newspapers are using now.

I know you're not an Orioles fan, but that's all they had at the police station. I asked.

I knew I had to work fast. I knew your blood type, of course, so I reached straight for the AB shelf. Then I hesitated because I didn't see any AB- hearts, only AB+, and I had to hurry up and look on my phone to see if you could even take that kind. And it wasn't until then, with all the frigid air rushing over my bare arms and chest, that I thought about how all those other hearts would go to waste because they wouldn't stay cold. Someone was going to come to the Organporium the next day and say, *I need an AB+ heart please*, and they wouldn't be able to get one because the whole case of them would be as questionable as egg salad left out on the picnic table all afternoon.

I realize now I could have just grabbed an O- and taken a chance. See, I'm O-, so I happen to know that that's the universal donor type. We O-s can give blood to anyone, and I plan to give everything to everyone when I'm gone. Take what you need and burn the rest, those are my final wishes.

Anyhow, I could have got out of there with an O- heart, but I couldn't stand the thought of all those other hearts going bad. So I started looking for something to cover up the display. I went into the back and rummaged around until I found some industrial strength Saran Wrap underneath a pile of insulated Organporium cooler bags, and I ran back out front and started wrapping up the case. That's when the police arrived. And I was so mad at them because the whole time they were questioning me, cold air was escaping, and those hearts were getting warm, and it wasn't until they led me out of the store that one of the officers found an insulated cover for the display case.

And now I'm calling you again, leaving you another message. They didn't count the first two toward my one phone call. I guess they only count the number of times you actually connect. And maybe that's where I went wrong. I thought I was building something with all my attempts to give myself to you, but none of that matters until someone actually takes your offering. That's the connection. But the unfortunate thing is, even though I could give my love to anyone, I only ever wanted to give it to you.

Not that you're counting, but this is actually call number four. My third call was to my friend Joe, who was standing ready just in case something went wrong and we had to go to Plan B. He got me out on bail, which wasn't too steep since I didn't hurt anyone and showed contrition by trying to wrap up all the merchandise. But you'd have known that, if you'd answered the phone.

Anyhow, doesn't matter, now. I'm calling from Joe's car at this very moment, and we're just a few minutes away from your place. I'm wearing my whisper-soft black ballet flats; and when you hear us at the last minute in the darkness of your bedroom, you'll barely even see me because I'm wearing a little black dress, just for you.

I wish I could be there to see you recover. My friend, he's a doctor of sorts. He says he'll take care of everything, and I trust him. I guess I'll have to, since I won't be around to make sure.

He didn't want me to call you, but I knew you wouldn't pick up, and that I'd just be leaving you a message. This is my last chance to tell you myself, tell you that I forgive you, and have never wanted anything but the best for you. And you may not be ready to hear it when you wake up from the procedure, but please know that everything that's about to happen is all for you.

I've always been right about what you needed. And I'm a universal donor, which means I can give my heart to anybody. But all I ever wanted was to give it to you.

Prior Publication Acknowledgments

"Death Sure Changes a Person" published by *Litbreak*, 2016

"New Growth" published by *T. Gene Davis' Speculative Blog*, 2015

"Aftermilk" published by *Booth*, 2017

"Another Damn Cottage" published by *Spelk*, 2017

"You, Commuter" published by *Jellyfish Review*, 2017

"Speculum Crede" published by *KZine*, 2016

"The Rapture" published by *b(OINK)*, 2017

"Midnight at the Organporium" published by *Heavy Feather Review*, 2018

About the Author

Tara Campbell (www.taracampbell.com) is a Kimbilio Fellow, a fiction editor at Barrelhouse, and an MFA candidate at American University. Prior publication credits include *SmokeLong Quarterly*, *Masters Review*, *Jellyfish Review*, and *Strange Horizons*. Her novel *TreeVolution* was published in 2016, followed in 2018 by her collection of fiction and poetry *Circe's Bicycle*.

Made in the USA
San Bernardino, CA
17 April 2019